EASTSIDE MÓRRÍGAN

(MIDLIFE SUPERNATURALS #3)

T.J. DESCHAMPS

EDITED BY
EMILY PAPER

EDITED BY
RHIANNON RHYS-JONES

This book is dedicated to The Coven: Erin, Emily, Silvana, Della, Sharon, and Christina.
Thank you for helping me raise my children, for supporting me through good times and bad, for having my back when I couldn't stand straight, and for showing me fierce loyalty and love.
I would not be the woman I am today if it weren't for your friendship, for the community we've created.
I love you as if you were my flesh and blood, more so.

We are the family we chose.

I also wanted to say something to a certain slug. This bog witch is glad you've entered my domain.

FOREWORD

Gentle Reader,

I am not a spiritual woman. The Mórrígan found me anyway a few years ago in Ireland. I was adrift, forgetting who I was, forgot my voice, my strength, and my joie de vivre.

She sank into my skin and became part of my flesh and bone. The goddess is not a gentle one. My life has changed drastically since she has guided me.

The Mórrígan released me now that I've paid for her help with this trilogy.

May remember who you are, to use your voice, find your strength, and rekindle your joy.

Best wishes on your journey,
T.J.

PROLOGUE

Sparks of electricity spiral down the length of my body, blooming at my core. Gabriel's mouth and tongue blaze a trail along the back of my neck and shoulder. His firm hand grips my thigh from behind, lifting my leg. We both gasp as he slides home.

He whispers, "This never gets old."

It really doesn't.

One year. It's been over a year since the first time we did this in a secluded cabin in the woods. It's *so* good. Every. Single. Time. Probably because the two of us making love without me bonding with Phyr can't last.

My faelight has grown.

Trouble will come.

For now, I relish his large body pressed into mine, the grip of his hand on my thigh, his breath hot in my ear, the friction of his length inside me lighting up every sensitive nerve. The ripples of pleasure build until it releases in a tsunami of sensation.

As I'm riding the residual ripples of pleasure, he asks in a raspy voice, "Tell me your true name."

I almost do.

The sex is that good.

My lips part, but nothing comes out. I can't tell him.

He pulls out and rolls over, sitting up on the edge of the bed.

My head and body are still trying to recuperate from the third mind blowing orgasm since we woke up, so I take a second to sit up and press a hand on his shoulder. "Gabriel, I love you."

I hope it's enough.

I know it's not.

"I know." He sighs. "I love you too, and that's the problem. You love me, but you don't trust me the way you trust Phyr, and that hurts."

Gabriel had a year to gain my trust. Phyr had many human lifetimes in faerie. It will never be the same, but I thought he'd gotten past his jealousy of my relationship with Phyr.

"Do you really want complete power over me?"

He turns. The face of the were-nephil is heartbreakingly handsome. Sometimes I get lost in how that beautiful face regards me. Gabriel looks at me as if I'm the best thing that's ever happened to him, and he can't quite believe I'm real. Right now, all I can see is the pain etched into those features, and I've caused it.

Although we've known each other for years, we've held a lot of secrets from each other. Naturally, when we started out, we didn't trust each other implicitly after discovering those secrets. We have a territory to protect and as protectors of our community, we are constantly faced with problems most people don't have. Sometimes we don't see eye to eye. Phyr has played a large part in keeping us together in more ways than one.

I hate that. I wish he were here to act as an intermediary. How are Gabriel and I going to work if we need my closest friend for every big argument?

Gabriel blows out his breath. If I look inside his head, I bet I'll see he's having the same thoughts. I could. I don't. I value his privacy too much.

His face is grim as he says, "Powerless? You could control me. Take over my mind and make me never disobey you."

Ah, there it is. Even the children of angels don't like someone having more power than them. They're almost like the cheesy '80s Highlander movies. *"There can be only one!"*

I get behind him, wrapping my arms and legs around his thick, muscular frame, and then rest my head on his shoulder. "Do you think I'd use that power over you?"

"No." He swallows hard, and I can feel he's not being completely truthful. "I already feel like I'd do anything for you. I've let high fae in this territory. I support you mate bonding with another because we're not compatible, and trust that won't break us. I am letting go of so much I wouldn't have let go before. I feel like if I had the name Danu gave you, it would be our way of bonding."

"Would getting married be a suitable alternative?" I don't even know if I want to do as I suggest. I was married once, and still might be technically married since Raf ascended to godhood, but I wonder if it would help Gabriel.

Gabriel stops breathing and grows absolutely still. Finally, he lets out a breath. "I would marry you in a heartbeat *if* you could commit to just me. As long as we're not married, the media doesn't question the nature of your relationship with Phyr. You two are never apart."

"Why is this bothering you now?" I gesture broadly, indicating everything metaphorically.

His shoulders heave. "The way we appear to the world matters."

I monkey my way around his torso to his lap. No small feat. I'm not a lithe halfling. "How would knowing my true name make a difference?"

His shoulders slump. "My enemies grow in number, but I can face anything, even death, if I know that you have that sort of faith in me."

Gabriel's sincerity moves me.

"It's not that I don't have faith in you. I don't trust my siblings." Maeve and Nix could pluck my name from his head as easily as plucking a stray hair. They are old. From a time when fae walked this world. Gabriel knows this. However, I don't want to point out that he's weaker than them. Not when he's in this vulnerable mood.

"Couldn't they do the same thing to Phyr?"

Fair point. However--"Phyr has a geas on his soul. Danu has bound him to never tell." I add in a soft voice, "No matter the torture."

His features darken. "They tortured both of you, didn't they?"

I nod, a sad smile forming. "Him more than me. Probably more so after I left."

"Bind me by geas."

I cock my head. "I don't think it can be done."

"It can." The resolution in his eyes tells me he's asked Phyr. He smooths a finger over my lip, pricking it on one of my fangs.

I taste the coppery drop of his blood.

"Tell me your name, and I'll swear on my soul to tell no one without your permission."

Magic settles in the room like fog rolling onto a meadow.

"My name is Mórrígan. Danu says I'm the goddess of old, reborn."

His eyes flash with surprise and his mouth gapes. He takes a few moments to recuperate from the news. His lips curl into a lascivious grin. "I love a battle goddess."

"That's a modern perspective. I prefer the role of protector and healer." I kiss his finger, pouring my faelight into it, healing the wound. Gabriel is a hemophiliac. He could draw from his pack to heal, but I want to emphasize my point.

His gaze drops to my lips. His hands slide down my back and grip my backside as his mouth finds mine. Gabriel kisses me with the fervor of a devotee at an altar, begging their goddess for succor. He breaks free of the kiss, leaving me panting. Cupping my face, he says as if swearing an oath, "I love you so much."

"And I, you."

It's true. I do love him, too, but I can't help the feeling that our love will be tested again. I can only hope that what we're building is rock solid enough to survive the coming storm.

CHAPTER
ONE

I didn't have opening Pandora's Box on my list of errands, but here we are.

A murder of crows that roost in the University of Washington Bothell campus fly overhead, darkening the evening sky as I make my way to check the mail. I hope they don't crap on my head. When a bird poops on you, it's supposed to be a blessing or lucky, but I think that's just wishful thinking.

A few of the crows break from the group, landing in the trees and on the mailbox.

One caws at me, likely expecting food. Sometimes I feed the crows unsalted peanuts.

I know. I know. I shouldn't be feeding wild animals, but I also feed cream to the sprites in my garden. I'm a sucker for all creatures. Actually, not all.

I don't feed Canadian geese. Those jerks can fend for themselves.

The crows remain at their posts, unafraid of my presence.

My mailbox is part of a huge communal locker of about forty individual boxes and two larger boxes for small packages. Busy with my bakery, I haven't checked the mail in about a week. I should punt the duty to my two acquired housemates, Rhiannon or Phyr, but I punt a lot to them so I can handle everything extraneous to the household. Besides, I like this being my task.

I have neglected mail for a bit, evidenced by the fliers, bills, and random junk stuffed tight.

A crow squawks so loud, I jump.

"I got nothing, buddy."

He takes off.

Fighting to work all the overstuffed mail out, I don't notice the prickle of unfriendly magic until it's too late. When I finally register something is amiss, I let everything drop. The contents of my arms fall to the wet pavement, cascading like autumn leaves. One envelope, however, sticks to my hand like a magnet to a fridge.

Like witchcraft.

While muttering a litany of swears that could make a sailor blush, I examine the envelope. Nothing out of the ordinary in the material, it's even weighted like a regular white envelope you might put a birthday card inside, except it's devoid of name or address. A tug of a compulsion spell urges me to open the envelope.

"Yeah right. I wasn't born yesterday," I say to the card because that's totally sane.

I was born to a witch and the High King of all fae, a long time ago. How long ago is anyone's guess. Nothing makes sense in faerie because it's all based on the beliefs of the fae who created it. If you aren't careful, that nonsense would kill you. Oberon, my father, always warned me to be aware of potential threats in even the most innocuous of settings. His advice kept me alive then, and I should heed it now.

"Miriam?"

I recognize the deep timbre of the voice and the worry. My neighbor Shawn made a promise to my late husband Raf to look out for me. Angels, like fae, take promises seriously.

I call over my shoulder, "Yeah. It's me."

Shawn comes into view under the streetlight. Judging by the

keys in his hand, he's come to check his mail too. I didn't hear his Tesla pull up, sneaky electric cars, but I see the sleek gleam of the grey sedan across the street now. He stands two heads taller than my average height of five-foot-six. Looks, build, and killer wardrobe included.

In contrast, I look like Molly Ringwald—2020's Molly, not the Pretty in Pink version. Well, if Ringwald had a thicker build. Much thicker. I've been a size fourteen to eighteen for a few years now. Also, I have antlers, fangs, and my hair decided to turn pink instead of gray, but I don't want to get into that. Going through fae puberty in my forties hasn't been fun.

Shawn's eyes are so dark that there's little difference between pupils and irises in the low light of the setting sun. He takes in the mess at my feet, and the envelope I hold as far away from my body as possible. He squints. "You alright?"

No. No, I am not alright. Not. At. All.

I'd thought coming out of the supernatural closet would solve my problems. Instead, I had to face down a religious cult and a witch coven entering this territory. Not to mention the members of the former Paradise Center cult have given me and the other council members grief for getting their elders sent to jail—none of the True Believers seem to mind that their leaders kidnapped my daughter and imprisoned me for the heinous crime of having the magic we were born with. Also, I still have the Angelic Anocracy to contend with but haven't heard from them. I'm not surprised. The long-lived take their sweet time to react to major shifts, swooping in when the dust settles. Hence the witches taking a full year to do this.

The envelope may be the first of many evils loosed against me in retaliation for blowing up everyone's spot.

"Fine. Fine. I've been supernaturally served. Nothing big."

Shawn rubs his hand over his short-cropped curls. "What does that mean?"

I cast a pointed glance in his direction. "I would think a former archangel and a current lawyer would know what 'served' means."

"I do. This—" He gestures to the envelope clinging to my skin. "—isn't the way the Angelic Anocracy goes about summoning for a trial. *Who* is serving you a summons?"

No. The Angelic Anocracy wouldn't do this. Gabriel said they will eventually send assassins with flaming swords to strike me, and the rest of the council, down. Especially after Gabriel and I brought down a cult devoted to them.

I sigh. Shawn is only trying to help. "When witches commit a crime against witches, the elders of all the covens meet. Once that committee decides the person needs to be tried, they send a summoning letter."

He listens, worrying his bottom lip. "Are you certain that this is what we're facing here?"

"*We*'re not facing this, Shawn. I'm going to figure this out."

He eyes me, grimacing. "We've been friends a long time, Miriam. Angels don't take friendship lightly. If you have a problem, I have a problem."

I take a deep breath. He's right. If the roles were reversed, I'd absolutely help Shawn any way I could. I've hidden what I am and so many secrets for so long, I'm still not used to having people have my back.

"Thanks."

He waves a dismissive hand while pocketing his keys. No mail pickup for Shawn.

A knot of guilt tightens in my stomach. He should be checking his mail and then driving around the block to his house, welcomed home by his kids and his husband Micah, not dealing with my family drama.

He eyes the envelope. "What will happen if you open it?"

"I assume opening it will activate a spell that will open a portal that will suck me to wherever a council of witch elders await to judge me."

More forehead rubbing. "Shit."

Shit is right.

I lick my lips, grinning. "There's always a chance Option B will happen."

His handsome face lights up with hope I hadn't meant to give him. "Which is?"

"The elders have already decided I'm guilty, and the envelope is a magical bomb."

I chuckle without humor. I'm panicking, and panicking will not get me out of this situation. Whatever I do, I cannot consider opening it. Not even hypothetically. Any intention in that direction will lead to the compulsion to do it.

A light blue BMW pulls up, a local punk band blaring from within. Kirsten, Roxy's mom, gave her a brand-new BMW for graduation, because of course she did. Just what I need. My kid is home from college.

My daughter Jada spills out of Roxy's car dressed all in black from her studded choker, My Chemical Romance t-shirt, ripped jeans all the way down to her Demonia platform boots. Her eye makeup and lipstick are dark, paling her brown skin. Her curly hair is currently teal, a halo around her shocked face.

"Mami, everything okay?" Concern colors her tone and her brown eyes are wide. Her expression shifts to excitement within a blink of an eye.

Jada reaches for the envelope. "Oh, that's for me!"

I whirl away, shouting, "Stay back!"

Her brown eyes light with the anger of a pissed off demigoddess. "Give it to me, mami. It's mine!"

Shawn puts himself bodily between my daughter and me.

"A compulsion spell coded for our bloodline is making you believe it's yours. Fight the urge," I say from behind the big, Graceless angel.

She furrows her brow and angles her head to the side, asking over Shawn's shoulder, "Do you want me to look up in the grimoire library to see if there's an unhexing I could do?"

"No. It's best if you and Roxy get as far away as you can. I don't know what this will do when triggered."

"I can feel the pull of a compulsion spell," she admits and then nods her head as if deciding something. "I'll get back in the car."

Roxy pokes her head out the window. "What's happening?"

"Call your father." Shawn says in a calm voice, "There's a magical terrorist threat, and we need his—"

"No!"

When they all gape at my shout, I add in a calmer tone, "I know what to do."

Shawn's brow furrows with concern, but he doesn't argue. He may have been a powerful seraph once, but all he can do now is sprout wings on demand. That's what "fallen from Grace" means, an angel stripped of magic.

Lucifer once told me what the Angelic Anocracy does to strip angels of magic. How they stripped him of magic. He eventually found a workaround-become the villain of the story. His power came from being the devil; not the fount the other angels' magical gifts sprang from.

Lucifer is also the reason I realized how to dismantle the magical bomb safely. Or rather, an encounter with him taught me something about faeries and their creators.

"What's the plan?" Shawn asks.

"Only what the fae believe can hold power in a faerie."

He cocks his head to the side.

"I'll explain after it's done," I say. "Right now, I need to get this thing out of here."

Light is what I call magical energy. Because my mother is a witch and my father is the king of the freakin' High Fae, I have a bit of witchlight, and a supernova's worth of faelight. Since fae are made of the stuff and I have a mortal body, I keep most of my faelight in what I call a cache. Caches are nulls, or the interstitial space between the fabric of the multiverse. I happen to have one inside me, or I can access it from there, but I don't like to think about it too much.

Quantum physics and magic make strange bedfellows but are bedfellows, nonetheless.

I take some of the faelight I have hanging around inside my cache and wield the magic like a blade to slice through the fabric of the multiverse, seeking my faerie.

"I'll be right back," I say and slip into my faerie.

Faeries rarely obey what we know as reality, because they are pocket universes based on the belief of the fae who created them. That is why the fae who could create faeries, called the High Fae, were worshipped by humans as gods.

Once inside my seedling faerie, I stand in a meadow, and the belief the envelope has no power against me makes the envelope becomes just that, a white unmarked envelope, dropping to the ground.

Spell broken, I create a flame with my faelight, burning the envelope to ash.

I sigh and turn around.

I am not alone.

A fae with bronze skin appears. I'm not using a fancy word for medium brown. His skin has a metallic sheen like a burnished bronze statue. Curling horns protrude from his silken black hair. His tresses are currently plaited away from his face. His face is all fae sharpness and ethereal beauty. Mundanes once worshipped his kind for not only fae magic, but their otherworldly perfection, which is a magic all its own.

Instead of the fae armor he wore in his own faerie, Phyr sports a pink t-shirt with our logo for the Enchanting Treats bakery we co-own. Flour dusts an apron with the same logo. His dark jeans are clean and so are the tattoos covering his arms. The mundane outfit should seem at odds with his faeness, but I'm used to it. Used to him. A smirk tugs at the corner of his sensual mouth as his amber eyes assess my predicament, or rather, lack thereof.

"Lemme guess. You sensed I was in trouble through our connection." I'd drank his blood more than once. Yeah. Drinking blood is gross. I know, but we still hadn't tied the fae bond knot and Gabriel and I are a thing.

"Although I appreciate how powerful you believe I am, Jada called me." Phyr's grin hikes up a few notches, to a smile that makes mundanes and supernaturals alike swoon. He flexes his fingers. "Feels good."

All magic is based on belief. The more people who believe in your gifts, the more you level up. I am sort of a goddess in this little pocket realm. My belief here is like getting a vitamin boost in your smoothie.

"I see you are no longer in dire peril and assume you already have the situation under control." It isn't a question. Phyr knows I don't do casual conversations in life-threatening situations. He's known me most of my life, except for the twenty-odd years we spent apart, thanks to my mother stealing me from faerie and hexing my memory.

I dust my hands off. "Thanks for showing up."

"A precaution, really." Gesturing to his lack of armor or sword, he adds, "I had no doubt I'd find otherwise. Still, Jada and Shawn voiced legitimate concerns. Something about a witch cursed letter?"

I explain the situation with the envelope. How it wasn't just a bomb scare. "As soon as they know this wasn't successful, there'll be more trouble coming."

His expression changes from mild amusement to one of cold malevolence. The way his voice remains casual with what he says next is beyond me. "Let her come. I am more than eager to settle her debt to our king."

To renege on a promise to a fae, especially the High King Oberon, my father, means death.

A frisson skitters down my spine. This is the side of Phyr I don't know well. The soldier who traveled back in time to fight angels. The planeswalker who could open a portal and use his telepathic abilities to convince his enemies to walk into the heart of a star. Phyr may be a prince of his faerie, but his duty is to act as Oberon's sword. After learning of how deep my mother's treachery ran, my father ordered her death. Since witches are supes, and have sided with Lucifer, she'd have no protection under Gabriel's bargain with Phyr.

Phyr extends a hand and changes the subject. "Shortcut home?"

I take it readily, realizing something as I do. "You have abilities in my faerie. Lucifer had none."

An 'ah, you noticed that did you?' grin touches his lips. "Firstly, you believe I have power here. Secondly, a planeswalker wouldn't be a planeswalker if a god's notion of what should or shouldn't be got in our way."

I don't like him referring to me as a god. The fae were once worshipped as such, but I don't like the idea of being worshipped...nor the yoke of my true name. "Huh. Good to know."

His expression is once again that of my friend. Mischief dancing in his amber gaze. "I'm stronger here than in any other place in the multiverse. Your faith in me knows no bounds and your faerie has no limits."

I don't have time to process because my stomach does a flip as he pulls me from the faerie into my living room.

Jada gives me a questioning look.

When I nod, indicating everything is fine, she leaps at me and crushes me in a Jada bear hug.

Shawn hovers, visibly relieved. "What happened to the envelope?"

"It lost all power in my faerie and then I burned it."

The former seraph's expression changes. "You're all-powerful in your faerie, like your father is in his domain?"

Judging by his tone, he doesn't like the idea. I don't know why he fell from Grace, but like every other fallen angel, including Lucifer, Shawn doesn't like the idea of any god but his.

"I suppose so," I reply, not giving up Phyr's secret. I can't be All Powerful if my friend can break rules.

Shawn's expression turns grim. "You should have killed Lucifer when you had the chance."

I roll my eyes.

"Yes, because it's all about angels and the fallen," Phyr replies, voicing my thoughts.

Shawn's gaze passes between the two of us. "If not Lucifer, who would put the witches up to this?"

I blink. Shawn is serious. Did he believe witches followed Lucifer blindly like the fallen and demons? We had a deal. We had our own agenda. I must stop including myself in that "we." I am covenless, a hedge witch.

"I stole and destroyed grimoires. That is the highest crime a witch can commit. I'm pretty sure the covens hate me all on their own."

"What about killing other witches?" Jada asks.

I shrug. "A new witch is born every day. Grimoires are irreplaceable. That was my coven's attitude, at least."

Jada wrinkles her nose. "Harsh."

The former angel shakes his head slowly, rubbing his short curls. "It may appear it's simply that. You don't know my brother like I do. If he can't defeat you himself, he'll deploy a war by proxy."

Shawn is right and wrong. Using others to work around the rules is Lucifer's usual tactic, but he knows that I'd link witches to him. Besides, Lucifer didn't want to fight me. He wants me at his side, bringing his brethren down a peg or two.

The witches were the ones to convince Lucifer to use the grimoires. They've had a grudge against male mundanes since the Middle Ages, when the church started burning us witches, and hapless mundane women, at the stake. The witch elders are likely spitting nails because I foiled their plans to exact revenge.

If they split from Lucifer, there's only one way to find out.

"I'll call Gabriel and discuss it with him."

Appeased I got a nephil on it, Shawn leaves.

CHAPTER
TWO

"I know you don't need me if you summon Lucifer in your faerie, but I want to be there," Gabriel says over the phone, after I explain all that's happened and what I plan to do next. "If that's okay with you?"

I shrug, even though he can't see me. "Sure."

Phyr lifts his eyebrows in surprise. He's seated on the sofa, reading. Even though I'm in the kitchen, his fae hearing can pick up both sides of the conversation. I know because mine's that good now.

Gabriel must share the fae's shock, because he exhales loudly, as if relieved. "Alright. When do you want to do this?"

"I could ask Phyr to fetch you right now, and we could meet in my faerie, if you like?"

I glance at Phyr. He looks up from his book and nods his assent.

After a pregnant pause, Gabriel says, "I prefer to drive over and leave from your place. Give me twenty minutes."

I agree and hang up. It hurts he doesn't want a door to my faerie opening in his house.

Phyr helps me collect the things I'll need to summon Lucifer.

"Part of me believes Lucifer wants this, that the whole thing is a setup to get me to contact him. Be on your guard."

My friend shakes his head. "No. I think he'd find another way. I believe the King of Hell no longer has a hold on the witches," Phyr replies. "Gracia would not take her time to exact revenge if he wasn't staying her hand."

"You're right." My chest feels tight. Despite my mother's betrayals, I just want to be free of her and hate that I have to go up against women I once loved and respected.

We enter the garden at the rear of the house. A now permanent nowhere door exists at the corner of the arbor. I could open a door to my fledgling faerie, but I'd rather save that for emergencies. Once a nowhere door is built, traveling by one takes no faelight. It's best to have all my resources whenever I confront Lucifer or go to a place that feeds on my light.

Walking through a nowhere door is never easy. The sensation of falling competes with my stomach doing flip-flops, and my eyes straining to see in a place without a source of light. I breathe easier once we're in my faerie.

I look to the sky, perpetual twilight because it is my favorite time of day. Yet the springy grass under my feet is a vibrant shade of green, as if it lives in full sunlight. Dogwoods and Sakura dotting a meadow are always in spring bloom, because spring is my favorite season. Jada was born on the spring solstice and it's a happy memory.

I briefly wonder if her father is in an impossible place like this or somewhere even more fantastical.

Phyr sets down the tray he carried for me and stretches out on the grass, tucking his hands behind his head.

I sit cross-legged next to my friend while I set out the bowl and knife required to summon Lucifer. As I reach for the candles to set up, Phyr yawns and closes his eyes. I quirk an eyebrow. "Are you going to take a nap?"

He cracks open an amber eye. A grimace tugs down the corners of his mouth. "That was the idea."

"I'm summoning the King of Hell, and you want to sleep through it?" I ask, rearing my head.

He opens both eyes. Amber gaze now intent on me, he lifts his eyebrows. "Why shouldn't I? I have nothing to say to him and you'll tell me whatever he says to you."

"If you're that tired, you can go home."

"I could." He smiles wide enough to reveal his fangs. Mirth twinkles in his amber eyes. "However, I'd rather rankle Lucifer. I'll wake up so much more refreshed, knowing my unconcern with his presence will no doubt stir his ire."

With an audible sigh, I say, "Real mature, Phyr."

His smile sharpens. "Is annoying him immature? Yes. However, I think you'd prefer it to what I'd rather to do."

I would probably regret asking, but I do anyway, "Which is?"

All humor leaves his features, and my heart skitters at the coldness in his usually humor-filled amber eyes. "What I'd like to do is take over his mind as I tear his feathers off one by one, and then break each delicate bone of his wings before ripping them off completely. Then, I'd stab my sword between his thighs and slice upward, keeping him alive with my faelight as I sever him in two at an excruciatingly slow space. All the while, I would not take my gaze from his beautiful face until nothing remained but twisted agony. Then, and only then, I'd say, 'I will wipe all memory of you from her mind and from all the minds of all who knew you so that when you die, all that you've done and all that you ever were will be forgotten.' before I relieved him of his long, long life."

"Phyr, I—" I choke on my words, too overcome with emotion to speak. I want to apologize for my part in causing his pain.

His hands find my cheeks, wiping away tears that fall unbidden. "You were a victim, molded to be who he wanted, not a participant. What he did to you, who you were at that time, was not you, not really."

If I look back with that perspective, none of what I felt for Lucifer was real. My mother and her coven convinced my impressionable mind that I had something of real value... when all I possessed was a gilded cage.

As I lift my gaze to meet Phyr's, tears sting my eyes. I say the unspoken among fae, "Thank you. Thank you for the pixies. Thank you for believing in me when I didn't even believe in myself. Thank you for being a faithful friend when you could have moved on and forgotten me completely. Thank you for putting up with Gabriel's rules. Thank you for supporting me through this transition. I don't deserve your undying loyalty, but I will endeavor to do so."

Danu's blessing and binding magic settles into my skin. I owe Phyr to be a better friend than I have been.

Phyr only stares at me, wide-eyed and slack jawed.

Deep in my gut, I feel a pull to lean forward and kiss him. Instead, I take the tip of my finger under his chin and close his mouth. "You'll catch flies."

He chuckles.

I poke him in the chest. "If anyone will kill Lucifer for what he's done to me, it will be me."

The grin takes on a new meaning as his lashes lower and his gaze settles on my mouth. Phyr's voice drops an octave. "Would it be uncouth to admit that imagining you slaughtering the King of Hell excites me—sexually?"

Heat floods my chest and other regions. The memory of the way he kissed me after I'd escaped the Paradise Center flashes in my mind, unbidden.

"It's a little sick, if you ask me," a deep voice rumbles behind me.

Pulse quickening at the sound of my current lover's voice, I turn. My breath hitches.

My beau Gabriel is, in a word, radiant. While Phyr's features are a study of angles and fine lines, the were-nephil's features are bold, and his mouth sensual. His green eyes are brilliant in the frame of tan skin and dark, curly hair. The archangel of the Pacific Northwest stands well above six feet tall. Lean muscle still apparent under a three-piece suit.

Phyr shoots over my shoulder. "I didn't ask you, nephil."

"We have an agreement, fae," Gabriel responds, leaning over to kiss my cheek. There's teasing in their tones, whereas a year ago they would be at each other's throat, quite literally.

I breathe in Gabriel's scent—evergreen forest, the spice I associate with angels, and fabric softener. Although we've never lived together, he smells like home. I tug his tie playfully. "What's with the suit?"

Gabriel tucks in his chin as if he forgot what he's wearing and sports a grimace when his face lifts again. "I've been approached by some high-powered shifters who would like me to run for political office."

My eyebrows hike up my forehead. Gabriel has connections high up in the political world, but archangels were supposed to stay out of mundane governments. "What did you say?"

"I listened and said I'll consider it," he replies, blowing out his breath. "These aren't the type of people I can refuse outright, if shifters are going to move out of the role of Guardians and into a position in society that's more ours."

My stomach knots.

Phyr strokes his chin. "If you were in the public spotlight, it would be harder for the Angelic Anocracy to assassinate you without repercussions. In the present, you're just a guy on T.V. As a beloved public figure..." The fae shakes his head.

Gabriel nods slowly. "A year ago, I'd turn them down. It's part of the Angelic Code for archangels to stay out of the public eye."

We'd blown that out of the water going viral when we came out as supernaturals on a local news station, and again when we appeared on an exposé.

According to Phyr, this is what the archangel had once wanted. Judging by the way Gabriel runs his hands through his curls and the frustration marring his handsome features, I don't think he wants that at all.

"They had good reason. Reps of the Pope, the Patriarch of the Eastern Orthodox church, and a few other religious leaders called, asking for my freakin' blessing? One pastor compared my exposing the Paradise Center to Jesus overturning the tables of the moneylenders and wanted to know if I was making way for the second coming of Christ." He shakes his head woefully. "No matter how I reply, belief in me grows stronger. This is not what I'd meant to do."

Phyr and I exchange a glance. Belief like that could make him a literal god. Gods could not exist on this plane, ascending to a higher form of life. Raf, Jada's father, had terrible cancer because a mortal body couldn't sustain the power of a god. No wonder he looks troubled. No one who values their family and community the way Gabriel does would want godhood.

"I'm sorry." I lay a comforting hand on his shoulder and squeeze. "That's rough."

Phyr has a look of respect on his normally mischievous eyes. "A lesser person would take all the credit and enjoy the enhanced power."

Sighing, Gabriel replies, "I know how this can change me. You two are the only ones I know who will tell me if I stop being me." The were-nephil meets the fae prince's gaze. "Especially you."

Phyr grins. "You are correct."

THREE

After the first droplet of my blood splatters the rim of a chalice, it takes the length of a single breath before dense tendrils of glittery smoke forms before me and Gabriel. He takes a ready stance as the smoke coalesces into a writhing pillar akin to the cypress in Van Gogh's "Starry Night."

With a flutter of dark wings, the smoke scatters, and Lucifer appears. Like any angel, the King of the Fallen possesses a face almost too beautiful to behold, and a body of graceful lines. His long hair and his eyes without sclerae or irises are solid black, but his wings are a navy blue so deep they seem black.

He takes me in the way one would take a long drink of water, slowly and savoring every drop. Then, his midnight gaze sweeps to Gabriel. His wings expand to their full-length, flapping once loudly —a direct challenge.

Shit. All I need is two angels losing their shit over me.

"I'm not here to fight you for Miriam," Gabriel says, holding his hands up.

Lucifer turns to me, his expression of utter surprise. "He doesn't claim you, Tati. How can you tolerate such weakness?"

My stomach twists. I was once a girl who would've taken his bait. There's no small amount of shame and regret flushing my face.

I'm not only embarrassed by the way past me behaved. A part of me feels pity for the King of Hell. He doesn't know me anymore and believes I would find his willingness to fight or claim me as something romantic rather than it being about me as his property.

Because I can't do much else lest insult him and find out nothing, I shrug. "I've summoned you as an ally. You said I could count on you as one."

A smile touches Lucifer's lips, expanding to a brighter smile than any mortal, or perhaps immortal, could wear. Angels are beautiful, but he is named Bringer of Light for a reason. His voice drips with honeyed overtures as he declares, "Anything for the love of my life."

Yeah. That's absolutely not the road I want to head down. This would be simpler if he didn't feel the need to outshine Gabriel in my eyes. It's juvenile for someone his age to act this way, yet immortals tend to get stuck in a stage of life instead of growing wiser. If immortals did try to improve, I bet they'd ascend to godhood.

"The witches have sent me a summons. I neutralized it. Do you know anything about this?"

Surprise limns his features. There and gone. He seems to puzzle out what I've told him for a few moments before replying, "Are you sure it was the witches? They know better than to go against me."

"I could see the witchlight in the spellwork."

"I see." His dark eyebrows gather in a scowl. Lucifer took every betrayal, every disobedience personally.

"Luce," I use my pet name for him, hoping to calm him a bit, "I think this is a matter between them and I. I wouldn't want you to act against the witches on my part."

"Perhaps someone hired a witch," Gabriel suggests. "Someone who would want you and your ally Lucifer at odds with your former coven. This needs to be investigated further."

The King of Hell dips his chin in agreement. "This is plausible, nephew. Acting against Tatiana in any way is forbidden. The covens may be furious about the destroyed grimoires, but they know the consequences of crossing m—"

A raucous snore drowns the rest of Lucifer's sentence. The King of Hell twirls toward the sound and gapes at the sleeping fae, asking with no small amount of incredulity, "Is that Prince Phyr *sleeping* on that knoll?"

"He was very tired," I reply.

Lucifer tilts his head. "He knew you were summoning me and decided it was an excellent time for a nap?"

I shrug, as if it is totally normal to have my so-called defender sleeping through my meetings with dangerous, ancient beings. "He didn't feel I needed him."

"Well, you do," Lucifer disagrees with a churlish look. "This could all be Unseelie Court nonsense meant to render you and I into opposition."

"He has a point," Gabriel agrees, heading toward Phyr. "I'll wake him."

Watching a bit of grumbling back and forth between Phyr and Gabriel, I jump as a taloned finger touches my arm.

Lucifer grimaces briefly at my reaction to his touch. "My brethren won't like the way Gabriel grows in power, his allyship with beings they consider lesser. Don't discount the angels using ruthless means to silence him."

I shake my head. "A witch wouldn't work with the angels."

"My brother Gabriel resembles me enough to fool a witch who is not used to my presence. Tell me you don't see myself in his son as well?"

"I don't." Pain ripples through me. I didn't think I had, but Danu's curse on lies hurts enough to convince me otherwise. Damn. Fae can't even lie to themselves.

Lucifer pinches his lips. "Still a terrible liar, Tati. One would think you'd learn from your fae servant."

Said fae servant approaches with Gabriel. The gaze of both centers on the proximity of Lucifer to me. Phyr shows no reaction, typical of a fae used to court intrigue. Gabriel's eyes narrow and his shapely mouth thins into a straight line.

Gah. Lucifer doesn't care about fae machinations and Phyr sleeping. He manipulated Gabriel and I so he could talk to me alone.

Irked, to the King of Hell I say, "So, you believe that either the fae or angels put the witches up to this?"

The fallen angel cuts me a look that says he's none too pleased I divulged our private conversation.

"No," Gabriel denies right away. "The angels wouldn't work with witches. Not after they've allied with you."

"Not every witch has allied with me," Lucifer retorts in a tone one would use with a toddler. "Surely, you know that."

I think of Rhiannon, the covenless witch, who moved into Gabriel's territory, escaping that allyship, and the Baba Yaga coven, who wants nothing to do with the rest of the covens. I push the thoughts out of my head. Phyr taught me to shield my thoughts, but I don't want to chance Lucifer knowing *anything* about my friend, who has slighted the devil by thwarting his crossroads demon's attempts at capture.

"Whether the angels would do such a thing isn't the question. Kidnapping Miriam by witchcraft wouldn't lead Gabriel to the angels." Phyr stretches languidly. "However, given the witches have motive to harm Miriam, such an act would create discord between Gabriel and the witches."

"Which my former coven wouldn't want." It irks me I haven't thought of that.

"I would believe it was them," Gabriel agrees.

I look around my ever-blossoming faerie, a sinking sensation dragging me down. "My siblings Maeve and Nix have access to witches and all kinds of supes in Nix's faerie."

Lucifer rubs his chin. "I am not on bad terms with your siblings. I could have my spies there investigate any sort of machinations Nix and Maeve are cooking up. You should pay some visits to the witches in your area. See how they behave in your unscathed presence?"

Not a bad idea. Not bad at all.

I AGREE.

CHAPTER

FOUR

After we part with Lucifer, I ask Gabriel over for dinner so we can discuss next steps. Roxy, his daughter, is already in my kitchen, cooking with Jada and my cousin, Niamh. Although my address is part of their official documents, Niamh doesn't actually live in my house. A water fae, they live in the nearby Sammamish River, also known as the Sammamish Slough, with their dragon familiar.

Niamh's features could never be mistaken as a human: they have white scaled skin with an iridescent shimmer, instead of hair they have silvery-white thin tubercles that help them sense things in water, black eyes without sclerae ,and nictitating eyelids over their eyes. The dark, translucent eyelid helps them adapt to above water light like sunglasses. Their thin slits for nostrils are for when they need to breathe air, and gills along their neck are for when they breathe underwater.

I'm glad my cousin has come over for a visit since we need to discuss my siblings' possible machinations. I frown at their choice of clothing, which is a dress of mine I was going to wear on my next dinner date with Gabriel. Niamh only sports clothes inside the house, so I guess it's a win?

Phyr and Gabriel get to work on setting the table. I oversee the dinner the trio are making.

Rhiannon and Lance, her boyfriend and Gabriel's pack gamma, join the group. The rock witch is a petite brunette. Like Phyr, she's still in her bakery uniform. "I'm going to catch a quick shower, babe," she says to Lance, kissing him on the cheek.

He smiles, revealing straight white teeth. Lance must have showered before picking up Rhiannon from work after his construction gig. His long, thin braids are loose and his dark and handsome face has that fresh-shaved looked. He's also in clean black sweats and a Seattle Kraken hockey jersey, which I know for a fact he wouldn't wear to work.

"Mind if I turn on the game?"

I smile and shake my head. "You might want to ask Phyr about using his television."

Lance nods to his alpha as Gabriel passes him.

My stomach flips as Gabriel picks me up by the waist, sweeping me into the laundry room and kicking the door closed behind him. My insides tie up with warm fluttering sensations as he sets me on the dryer and leans in. Our faces are level this way. His breath fans my face.

"Hi," he says, inhaling deeply.

"Hello handsome." My voice is breathier than I anticipated.

A panty-soaker smile graces his shapely lips. "Can I have a kiss before someone in this house realizes I've succeeded where others have failed?"

I hesitate. We've been playing with fire by being intimate without me bonding with Phyr.

His dark eyebrows draw together. "One little kiss can't hurt, right?"

I fork my finger into his hair at the back of his head, drawing his lips to mine. Gabriel's green eyes flash with surprise and then close as our mouths meet.

His hands cup the plump cheeks of my rear and squeeze as he presses the hard length of his body into mine.

One little kiss, eh?

Deep in my belly something stirs. Okay. A lot of things are stirring inside me, but the ravenous hunger building has nothing to do with sexy time and everything to do with a claiming only a fae is meant to survive.

I break off the kiss, pushing Gabriel away.

Worry limns his features. "Did I do something wrong?"

I shake my head. "You have a serious lack of awareness of exactly how much I'm attracted to you and how dangerous that attraction is." I've only tried to devour him once, but once is enough.

He nods, giving me a bit of space. "I've said I'm good with the two of you bonding and—" He blows out his breath in an audible whoosh, thick fingers combing through his brown curls. "—whatever may transpire during the course of it."

"As long as you're part of it, you can't be. My father disabused Phyr and I of the notion. He did say you can..." My voice trails off. I'm not prepared to have this conversation right now.

"Be there but not part, I know." Gabriel sighs. "It doesn't bother me. Does it bother you?"

"When we went to Nix's faerie, there was this fae. Their name is Fand. Phyr admitted he would have bonded with them, but he thought they died."

"Have you talked to him about it?"

I shake my head. "A little. He says whatever he felt is over, but I can't believe that. I think he should at least hear Fand out."

Gabriel smiles ruefully. "Nothing you did between leaving faerie and reuniting with him made him lose faith in you. Phyr knows his mind and his heart. If he truly wanted to bond with someone else, don't you think he would have done so?"

"There are court politics at play. He had to bond and have children with someone from my house, it was his duty. Phyr even said when he originally came here that he did so to protect his family."

Gabriel's smile changes. He taps my forehead. "This is getting in your way."

He turns to open the door. My cheeks flush when I see Phyr standing there as if he's been waiting.

"Your thoughts are loud, nephil. Can you not scream in my head," Phyr drawls with absolutely no bite. "Here I am, as requested."

"We have the rare opportunity for all three of us to discuss the bonding ceremony," Gabriel replies. "Miriam worries there's another you'd rather bind yourself to."

The fae prince enters and closes the door behind him. "I've told you, Miriam, I'd once considered bonding with Fand, but not why. War sometimes creates powerful feelings for your fellow warriors and not the enduring ones that last in times of peace. Emotions run high when life balances on a honed blade. Seeing Fand was a shock, and their betrayal a sting, but do not mistake my reaction to seeing them again as grief for a lost love. Despite my previous closeness to them, they were truly dead and mourned in my mind a long time ago. Quite frankly, I haven't even thought of them in what might be the equivalent of decades."

This information, on one hand, is a great relief. On the other hand I feel a deep sense of grief for the fae trapped in Nix's faerie. How many other fae in that bar, in Nix's entire faerie, have been forgotten by people who once loved them?

"It pains me fae are under indentured servitude in a time when there are so few, but they are not the matter we're discussing," Phyr replies to my thoughts as if I've spoken out loud.

I've drunk enough of Phyr's blood that I can barely shield my friend from my head. When we bond, all our thoughts and emotions would be laid bare to the other. It dawns on me the Phyr I knew as a child and the Phyr who has lived under my roof and has been my partner in business for the past year would not want to bond with someone who abandoned him during a war. It also occurs to me that *I* am the only one holding back the ceremony.

Phyr slides past Gabriel, touching my almost full formed antlers. A shivery sensation travels down my spine at the touch. The hunger deep in my gut stirs. We lock gazes.

"You must speak to Oberon. If your siblings have employed a witch for the spell, it's an assassination attempt, an act of war on the heir."

"Fun. I have a new threat to consider."

"It's not new," Phyr corrects. "Just dormant for a while."

Gabriel shakes his head. "Never a dull moment in the supe community."

"Speaking of threats, we should not hesitate on the bonding. You will be stronger for it," Phyr adds.

Gabriel nods in agreement. "Maeve or Nix alone might not be able to create too much damage, but two ancient fae after you is trouble supes don't need. The sooner you two get the ceremony over, the better."

I flush. "Well, let's see if my siblings are behind this first and then talk about the ceremony later."

My lover and my closest friend exchange a glance. I'm hedging and we all know it. Still, they let it be. I'm glad they're allowing me time to adjust while reminding me bonding is in my best interest. Whether it benefits me or not, this ceremony will change our dynamic. I'd like it to stay the way it is for a bit before delving into something new.

CHAPTER
FIVE

O beron joining us for dinner turns everything more
formal, but I need my father's advice on what to do
about my sibling's possible machinations.

After dinner, I regale the table with what happened with the
letter, adding Lucifer's input, and leaving out Phyr's nap for his sake
in front of his king.

"It is true. I have freed your siblings of their promise." Oberon
twirls a glass of a Washington cabernet and takes a sniff before
drinking.

"They wouldn't really kill mami, would they?" Jada asks, dark
eyes luminous and her brown skin paling a shade or two.

Oberon studies his granddaughter before replying, "They would,
my dear."

"You said there are not as many fae as there once were," Jada
protests. "Historically, wars are fought over resources or land. When
a fae can make their own faerie and there are so few fae, why would
they want to fight my mother and why would you condone such an
action?"

I wondered the same thing my entire childhood. The entire table stops eating and turns to the king of the fae.

Oberon sets his wineglass on the table, then pats the corner of his mouth. "I condone nothing. With the exception of your mother, my children are ancient, my dear, and therefore powerful enough to disobey me. Perhaps they may even take arms against me as well. They have supporters aplenty. Nix and Maeve wish to seal all nowhere doors to Earth and not venture into this world again."

"Nix made a faerie with a nowhere door to Earth," I protest.

My father scoffs. "Nix made nothing. That faerie is on conquered soil. A fae lordling died so your siblings could play at running a faerie."

I shiver and exchange a look with Gabriel and Phyr. Even with very few fae left, my father didn't punish his children for murder. I don't know if Oberon is being indulgent or if the number of supporters my siblings have garnered troubles the king.

Gabriel, sitting at the opposite end of the table, turns to Phyr. "Could you destroy the nowhere door between Earth and Nix's faerie?"

Sitting next to me, Phyr shakes his head, regret limning his features. "I could, but I won't. Collapsing a nowhere door would trap all the fae in there eternally."

Oberon clears his throat. Once all eyes turn to him, he says, "What I can say about my children is that employing a witch to do their work is as unlikely as it is probable. However, they bear much ill will towards witches and would not disregard the potential threat of your mother as the one who sent you the ill tidings. Gracia fears Lucifer not, or she wouldn't have placed that hex tied to a geas binding your light."

"I'm starting to think that Lucifer had a point, too," Gabriel admits. "All it would take is one angel who wanted to get to me through you. If I were chasing you down wherever I believed the spell took you, they could kill me and place the blame on witches. My death would leave my territory open to an archangel to take my place and vilify witches to all supes all in one blow."

So many powerful factions want me dead. A band wraps around my chest, squeezing; and the room seems suddenly smaller. I scramble to identify five things which I can see and take a drink of water—techniques I learned from my supe therapist. Panic wouldn't do when I had many potential enemies at my door.

Oberon turns his green gaze on Niamh, commanding in high fae, "I want you to pay your cousins a visit. Learn all you can along the way."

The water fae's thin mouth widens. "I will bring Báirseach."

"You're going to bring borscht?" Rhiannon asks, speaking for the first time in a while. "I love the stuff!"

"Báirseach is the name of Niamh's dragon," Phyr provides, stressing the pronunciation "bahr-shah."

Gabriel grimaces. He approved Báirseach to live in this territory as long as the dragon didn't harm humans, but he didn't like the idea. I convinced him they had sentience and self-preservation instincts. Báirseach understood humans are the dominant species in this world. The dragon isn't stupid enough to harm one.

"We should pay the covenless and the Baba Yaga coven a visit and see what we can learn," I suggest to Rhiannon.

Jada and Roxy exchange glances. Roxy nods to some silent agreement. "We can talk to supes on campus and in the city. The younger generation aren't as entrenched in old beefs and might spill the tea more readily."

"I'd like you to stay away from the Fremont Troll," I warn, knowing full well I can no longer prevent my college-aged daughter from doing anything dangerous. "That nowhere door leads to Nix's faerie. I don't want you trapped somewhere you can't escape."

"Granddad says if I want to get to know them, they won't hurt me because I'm Phyr's heir, not his," Jada replies, pushing her food around her plate.

I cut "Granddad" with a sharp glare.

"If you want to venture into the Bizarre Bazaar, you may accompany me," Niamh offers in halting English. They've been learning the language fairly quickly since coming to this world.

Both young women perk up.

Gabriel blows out his breath. I seem to not be the only parent struggling with this. "Will nothing less than a direct order change your mind, Box-o-Rox?"

Roxy purses her lips and rests her hand on her face, tapping her temple as if considering his question carefully. "Hmmm... how does that hold up to the 'I will never threaten you or give you a direct order' promise?" Her sarcasm is replaced with an ice-blue glare. "I'll answer. Not. At. All."

Oberon smiles, revealing a bit of fang. "What a lovely child. An excellent companion for you, granddaughter."

The girls and Niamh take off shortly after Oberon returns to his faerie. I watch the three of them go from the front porch, post dinner coffee in hand. Gabriel circles his arms around my waist from behind and places a kiss on my temple.

His body and tenderness warm a little of the chill settling in. Facing so many factions who want me, Gabriel, or both of us dead isn't exactly what I'd expected when we came out of the supernatural closet.

He murmurs, "If it's any consolation, I hate that they're going and we can do nothing about it, too."

That much was obvious at dinner, but I hold my tongue. "I feel like in my attempt to solve my problems with Lucifer, I've created a myriad more."

"The witches would have eventually found you. Your siblings were waiting for you to mature, but the fae who want to have a relationship with Earth and the fae who want to stay in isolation already had their beef. The angels have held complete power too long and the balance of the universe is out of order. Shedding light on something that oppresses a group doesn't cause problems. It just makes the problems which already exist harder to conceal."

Gabriel is right. Still, I can't help but feel to blame. I turn and kiss him, easing some of the troubled thoughts.

If only for a little while...

CHAPTER
SIX

I rise before dawn, readying for work. When you own a business, you can't take an entire day off to play sleuth, figuring out who attempted to kidnap or murder you the day before. After having the privilege of being a stay-at-home mom, giving the witches who have young children evenings and weekends off as much as possible is important to me.

Phyr, Rhiannon, and I open the shop and do our prep duties with our usual banter. We've been at this business for almost a year now and work well together.

Once prep is done, Phyr and I have a special order of Seattle Kraken cupcakes on a long table. A talented artist, the fae prince is better at intricate work, so I do the base frosting and then let him do the details of the design.

"I have something to tell you two," Rhiannon begins, wringing her apron. "I would have said something at dinner, but I was too nervous around your pretty father to say anything."

Phyr snorts. "I'm certain the high king would appreciate that you think of him as pretty."

She shoots him a nervous glance and wrings her hands. Then her gaze returns to me. "Well, I might as well say it. Lance, Daystar, and I found an apartment. Lance is swinging by to get my things after work."

I never planned on taking on another witch in my household, but Rhiannon was a welcome addition to my life. I'm going to miss our chats and ritual spell work. Her presence has made transitioning into an empty-nester easier. Pushing aside my own feelings about losing a housemate, I smile and say, "Congratulations!"

"Yes, congratulations," Phyr says, taking my cue. He seems a bit lost though why we're congratulating her.

I'll likely have to explain later. For now, I hug Rhiannon to show her more enthusiasm. She's come a long way from the feral witch we found up in Wallace Falls, and moving to her own place with her partners *is* something to be celebrated.

The rock witch lets out an audible sigh of relief as we embrace. "I thought you wouldn't approve."

I step back. "Why ever would you think that?"

She worries her lip. "Daystar's mother is livid that he's leaving."

It takes me a moment to register that she's comparing my relationship with her to the mother-son relationship of Ezmal and Daystar.

"You're a grown woman, and I'm certainly not your mother." Not to mention Rhiannon is over ten years older than I am.

The bell in the front rings, alerting us that there's a patron to attend to.

"I'll get it!" Rhiannon exclaims, rushing to the front.

Phyr and I lock gazes. With Jada at college during the week and some weekends, it would be only he and I come Monday.

His throat works and something akin to anxiety fills his eyes.

"I don't bite," I tease. "We'll find something to occupy our time."

"Remember when we were children, and you and I would play in your father's wood?"

"We pretended to be queen and consort," I say, remembering the

39

game—a precious memory regained after Rhiannon broke my mother's hex.

"I promised to bond with you then because I've loved you and wanted to be your bondmate since the first moment I laid eyes on your fiery hair and spotted skin, covering an indomitable spirit."

He approaches but doesn't crowd me. "If I'm honest, I still want to be your consort. I would like for us to know each other in every way, to be intimate in every way. Bonding would mean to me to remain at your side as your lover, friend, and advisor. I will accept if you wish it to not be so, but I think it would be best if I moved my belongings to Gabriel's home. He said I could if you didn't accept."

It stung when Rhiannon said she was moving out. The thought of Phyr living anywhere but with me robs my lungs of air. I've been procrastinating our bonding because something about it didn't feel right. Now I know why I hesitated. Remaining platonic wouldn't work. I couldn't just sleep with him once.

Finally, I find my voice. "I accept."

His dark eyebrows knit. "Because you don't wish to live alone or because you desire me to stay?"

"Does it matter?"

"If you have to say that—"

My eyes sting with unshed tears. "I don't ever want to live apart from you again."

"Why is that?" He closes the distance between us but doesn't crowd me. "Are you afraid of living alone?"

"Because I love you," I reply sincerely.

The archangel is my lover, but there's an irreplaceable history between Phyr and I. Even recently he left his faerie, his life, to be with me and Jada, adopting her rather than holding me into a creepy breeding agreement between our families. Phyr even played my guide with the relationship between me and Gabriel, a former enemy of his. All he's done is sacrifice for me. How could I not love him?

Phyr smiles and it's not a pretty one. "I know. You love the boy who suffered your every whim."

"No, not just the boy who played consort in the wood and had my back at court, but the grown fae who has been my partner in every way for the past year."

He sighs. "In every way, save one."

"True."

No wonder he wants to leave. With my house less hectic, Gabriel might be over more often. It isn't fair Phyr acts as my partner in business and home, but I deny him the intimacy that I want too, fearing I'll lose Gabriel.

Phyr moves closer. "Do you want me as a true consort?"

My heart pounds in my chest, threatening to burst through bone and flesh. "Yes."

He cups my face, brushing my tears away. "Then we should bond as anam cara, not for protection from our enemies or so you can have sex with Gabriel, but for the love, the friendship, and devotion we feel for each other."

My hand trembles as I place it over his heart. The rhythm steadies me. Phyr steadies me.

"Okay. But I—I don't want to be monogamous again." I don't want to give up Gabriel is what I don't say.

A grin curves Phyr's mouth. "That is a tradition of the short lived so that they have someone to care for them in old age. I hold no jealousy in my heart. Have as many lovers as you wish."

I laugh. "There's only one other. I don't want a harem, Phyr."

"We'll need to discuss this with Gabriel—Also, he and I need to discuss something with you."

My stomach flutters. "Such as?"

He leans in, breath fanning my face. "I'm not at liberty to say without the were-nephil present."

"Is it about a v becoming a triangle?" I ask, flushing hairline to chest.

His eyes glitter with absolute mischief and, I think I have my answer.

"You're adorable," he declares, kissing the tip of my nose. "We need to finish this order."

RHIANNON ENTERS THE BACK ROOM, a wry grin on her face. She does a plié and then gets on her tip toes and spins around, finally extending her hand in my direction. In a fake British accent, she says, "Your Highness, a courtier awaits in the oubliette."

I cock my head to the side, confused. An oubliette was a small dungeon. My father had many in his castle, but we didn't have anything of the sort in the bakery. "What?"

She groans and throws up her hands. "Ugh. You have a fancy dude in the front and he's looking for the heir of Oberon."

Phyr and I exchange glances. Gabriel allowed fae in the territory. Most fae loathe modern cities and suburbs, sticking to the vast forests of the Cascades and Olympics. They're supposedly here looking for someone to take back to faerie to have children with but are worse than a socially awkward teenager at getting one.

I assure the fae who come here that there are mundanes who would be happy to oblige. They usually stick their noses up at the fae groupies I show them on social media. Fetishization of fae is uncouth to the ancient fae, apparently.

A few of the younger fae find the fan groups amusing and take them away as faerie brides or grooms, bringing them back to Earth rather quickly. The reality of my father's faerie isn't as sexy as it is romanticized in fiction. Some settle in my faerie as a compromise. It's tamer than Oberon's faerie but something can be said for modern plumbing of Earth over brownies clearing out your commode.

As I exit the back to greet the newcomer, I hope this one isn't a suitor. I've had a handful of those and it's as awkward as you think it might be to navigate fae manners and reject someone without offense.

It is a fae lordling, judging by his clothes—a lace cravat, brocade waistcoat and jacket, and silk breeches with buckled shoes. Mint green hair is plaited down his back. His features are elegant. Power emanates from him. He's old. Oh boy.

He bows with a flourish. In lightly accented English he says, "Princess Tatiana, I offer my fealty."

It feels rather formal for a greeting in a bakery. There are two clients waiting for their order at the side, gaping.

"I welcome you to the Pacific Northwest, Lord—"

His gaze sweeps to where Rhiannon boxes the other client's order.

The rock witch shrugs. "Lord Farquat?"

A scowl wrinkles his brow, there and gone. "Lord Feidhil, at your service."

I grin at the name meaning beauty. "I'm pleased to make your acquaintance."

"I seek a bride. I would like to provide for her a comfortable home and hearth here in her homeland so that she may be comfortable as we begin a new line for my house." His arm disappears as he reaches into a cache, producing a bag. It looks hefty and laden with gold coin. "I'm told this trifle would be enough to provide for my future family."

I give him the name and address of Gabriel's liaison for the fae, a map of the neighborhood with directions.

"They are a shapeshifter, but they are allied with me," I say, not for the first time dealing with a newly arrived fae. "You may make any appointments with me through them."

"You are so kind, Princess Tatiana. I hadn't hoped for much, but this is exceptional." He sketches a bow before leaving.

"That," a client says, panting, "was the hottest man I've ever seen."

"Was he for real about a bride and buying her a house with a bag of riches?" Her companion asks.

I nod. "Fae men cannot lie."

She sprints out the door, followed closely behind by the other.

Rhiannon throws up her hands. "They forgot their cookies!"

CHAPTER
SEVEN

I pull the Enchanting Treats delivery truck into the parking lot of a Renton apartment complex and engage the brakes. Since my antlers have added four or five inches to my 5'6" height, I drive the delivery truck more and let Rhiannon drive my Subaru.

With my encouragement, and Gabriel's government connections for a fake birth certificate and social security card, she got her first driver's license. Rhiannon went from feral rock witch, living in a faerie forest, to an employed, housed, and tax-paying citizen in a year and a half. I couldn't be prouder.

In hindsight, I've been preparing Rhi to move out for a while. It still stings that she's moving out today. I also could have used a backup for what I'm about to do. However, the covenless witch visits need to happen now before news spreads that the trap didn't work, so I can catch a genuine reaction. If any witches in my territory are behind the magical letter bomb, they'll be shocked when I show up intact on their doorstep.

The visit goes well, likely because I've brought pastries and a couple of plant starters for the hearth witch's balcony. The second visit goes well too. All the visits reveal nothing other than witches eking out a new life without covens.

I pull into my driveway, knowing there's one more road I need to explore. For that, I'll need Phyr.

When I get out of the delivery van, I spy Lance's truck in the cul-de-sac. Everyone who works for Gabriel's construction firm seems to drive trucks.

Lights as small as fireflies, if Washington had fireflies, dance around me in greeting. The pixies flit back and forth. Fortunately, they have no bad news for me.

In the house, Roxy and Jada sit at the breakfast bar. Phyr has served lunch and sits with them. Rhiannon stands with a plate, as do Lance and Daystar.

Phyr makes to get up.

I urge him to sit. "Finish. I can plate my own food."

"So, how did the Bizarre Bazaar adventure go?" I ask the kids. Yeah, they're in college, but I still think of them as *my* kids.

"That place is so—" Jada begins, entire face lighting up.

"Scary," Roxy finishes, cutting her a sharp look. To me, she says, "I can't believe you have the same father as those fae."

"My siblings are pure malice, but Oberon has earned his own reputation," I reply. He's not the sweet grandfather they know, but I don't elaborate on just how terrifying my dear ole dad could be. Best to leave that emotional damage behind. "Define why the twins were scary."

If my siblings threatened my child, grown demigoddess or not, I would make them pay.

"Maeve and Nix could tell Roxy had angelic blood," my daughter explains. "I told them she was cool and not into the whole extermi-nate-all-fae thing. They were super nice to her, but then said we had to leave for our safety."

Judging by Roxy's expression, she didn't buy the fae's protector act. "Seems fae aren't the only ones who hate angels. Can't believe

I'm getting shit for something I don't even have anything to do with."

"Angels have abused their power. Like it or not, some supes will hold ill will toward you regardless of what you do. Don't take it personally," I say, knowing a lot of supes don't like fae or witches.

Roxy runs a hand over her close-cropped hair, muttering something about the threat feeling personal.

"The trip wasn't a complete waste," Jada says, glancing at Roxy. "Maeve and Nix didn't send the envelope. They were super offended that you thought they'd act so cowardly."

Roxy snorts. "Yeah. Maeve said they wouldn't want to miss devouring the light leaving your body when you die. Real charmer, that one."

I smile at Roxy, handing it to the kid for seeing through the fae charm.

"I don't think Nix wants to kill you. I think they just don't want to get in another fight with the angels," Jada offers. Her expression and tone turn solemn. "Grandfather believes you're some sort of key to peace and prosperity for the fae, but Maeve and Nix think that you'll bring the end to all fae."

It's so wonderful to hear from your kid the terrible things your siblings think about you. I see a note of fear in her eyes and chew my lip. I could work with this information. Maybe. I don't know how to abate my siblings' fear when my actions have caused discord with the angels. At least I know why they hate me, and it isn't about me being the heir.

Our ears are suddenly assaulted by music as someone's cell buzzes.

"Is that Boss Bitch by Doja Cat?" Jada asks, laughing between words.

"Princess's ringtone, I bet," Roxy quips with a snort.

Lance cusses and pulls out his cellphone from his sweats. He answers, "Yes, beta." His muscles tense and his face pales as he listens.

A year ago, the shifter could have carried a private conversation with Princess. With fae hearing, I pick up Gabriel's second in command's urgent tone. Naturally, I'm curious and focus on the tinny phone speaker.

"—the cubs refused to shift back into human form to speak—they've been through so much. I didn't want to force them. Gabriel's scent stopped nearby, but I found no trace of him. I picked up unfamiliar scents too, and magic, witch magic. I'm calling Miriam next to see if she can figure out what kind of spellwork is at hand."

Lance's dark eyes fixed on me. "I'm at her house—I think she heard everything."

I bob my head, indicating I had. Gabriel had taken the pack cubs for a hunt. The group split up. The adopted cubs and Gabriel didn't return with the rest of the party. Princess checked the compound's forest cameras and found her cubs, but no sign of Gabriel.

"I'm coming right away," I say, though I feel tired to the bone from a hard day's work and sleuthing.

"I'm coming too," Jada and Roxy chime in.

"We'll all go," I agree. "The council needs to be alerted, too."

CHAPTER

EIGHT

Gabriel's house is set in a posh, heavily wooded area of the Eastside. These types of homes you can't see from the road, with gates where you need to be buzzed in. His property has acres of lush forest with wild game, greenhouses, stables, and a mansion built in the style of a farmhouse. I wait in the parking area in front of the house with Princess and her girlfriend Aurora while Phyr gathers everyone from the council. Lance, Rhiannon, Daystar and a few familiar shifters, namely Syd and Nate, stand off to the side. Roxy and Jada linger close to me.

Princess's dark hair is swept in a ponytail. She wears no makeup. Her badass-biker-chick look is swapped for deep gray leggings and a tee—the uniform of Pacific Northwest moms.

Aurora wears the same sort of clothing, except her leggings are rainbow tie-dye and her hoodie is a cheerful yellow with green mountains behind a brown silhouette of a bigfoot on the front. Above the bigfoot on the hoodie, it reads in bold green print: "I BELIEVE".

Of course, she believes. Aurora *is* a bigfoot under the glamour of a tall, willowy blonde.

Lucinda is the first of the arrivals. She's about my age and gets her dark curly hair and large brown eyes from her Puerto Rican father, and elegant features and compulsion magic from her siren mother. Compact and athletic, she stays in fighting-shape for Persephone's army by training and competing in triathlons. She's in a polo with her cafe's logo and slacks, still dressed for work.

Next comes Leilani, a Hawaiian demigoddess. Leilani towers over most of the shifters. She's still in her white lab coat with a stethoscope around her neck. A physician at a clinic that is open twenty-four hours, she was likely working the night shift.

Shortly after her, Leilani's leprechaun fiancé, Cian, appears. He's in casual clothes, likely having finished at his construction job and relaxing at home like I had been. He rubs his strawberry blonde hair and blinks as if he's trying to wake up.

The advantage of having a planeswalker in your midst is that you can move a lot of people from different locations to a single point quicker than mundane means of transportation. Popping up in the members of the Supernatural Council of the Pacific Northwest's houses, places of business, and a busy restaurant is a bit rude and the cause of a lot of jump scares, but they all get over it when they hear *why* Phyr showed up.

Once all are gathered, Princess gives everyone the same story she gave us over the phone.

"I'm sorry your dad is missing. You'll have to act as interim archangel until your father is found," Lucinda says to Roxy.

Roxy's kohl-lined blue eyes gaze back at us, wider than usual. A grimace replaces the usual smirk on her dark purple painted lips. She wrings her hands. "Okay, I guess."

Princess jabs a finger at Roxy. "Being acting archangel is a privilege as well as a duty. Take this seriously, Roxanne."

A pulse of magic from the were-honey badger pricks my skin.

Roxy cuts Princess a glare, eyes flashing gold. "Try me with that wannabe alpha compulsion b.s. again and find out who's the real alpha here. Just like your daddy."

I shake my head, scowling in disapproval. That was a low blow, bringing in how Gabriel had to killed Princess's father.

A low, preternatural growl rumbles from Princess's throat. Her face hardens. "Until we find your father, I *am* the alpha, and you will respect me."

Roxy scoffs. "You got to earn my respect. So far, you've failed to compel me or do anything, really."

Lucinda steps her petite frame in front of the tall and muscled beta. I follow suit, standing in front of my daughter's best friend.

"Is this how we want to conduct ourselves with enemies in our midst?" Lucinda asks, her Spanish accent thicker with her distress, "like posturing alphaholes?"

Roxy opens her mouth to speak. Knowing the teenager for most of her life, I can already hear her say, *"She started it."*

I shake my head slowly before the words slip from her mouth. If Roxy wants to be treated like an adult, she needs to act like one. Starting by realizing she can't control what Princess does but can control her reactions.

The were-nephil clamps her mouth shut.

Princess lets out an exasperated breath. "I'll acknowledge Roxanne as acting archangel and give her the proper respect, if she acknowledges me as alpha of the pack and does the same."

Roxy pinches her mouth tight. For a few tense breaths, I believe she's going to decline and we're going to have a fight on her hands. Her mother, Kirsten, set a terrible example of behavior, throwing tantrums and starting fights with other women out of jealousy.

It's harder to make the right choice when you've never seen the right choice in the person you look up to the most.

Roxy blows out her breath. "I agree to the interim alpha's terms."

Pride swells in my chest as tightness eases from my shoulders. Jada, who stuck by Roxy's side, releases an audible sigh of relief. The air lightens as everyone recovers from the tension. Only a fraction, though. Gabriel is still missing.

"I propose all able-bodied shifters and demigods shift into

animal form, canvas the woods in groups to sniff out any clues," Princess begins, glancing at Leilani and Jada. "We don't know if they set up more traps, so be wary. Witches and those who can't shift into animal form will accompany me to the place where Gabriel went missing. Are we in agreement?"

We are. The group breaks up into two parties. More shifters pour out of the house, likely already aware of Princess's plan. I watch Roxy organize the shifter, demigod, and cryptid hunting party. Aurora is among them. The bigfoot doesn't shift, but she has a strong sense of smell and lived a good deal in the forest.

That leaves Lucinda, Cian, Phyr, Rhiannon, Daystar, and me to follow Princess. She leads us past the house down a trail that cuts past the greenhouses and stables to the wood. The air is fragrant with the scent of trees towering at least one hundred feet above us. The common Douglas Firs are not the only trees I can smell. Moss covered Western Hemlocks, Sitka Spruces, Ponderosa pines, and Western red cedars all populate this forest, and most of Western Washington. The varieties of trees and moss earn the state its nickname, The Evergreen State. Soft packed mulch lines the trail, ferns and tangles of blackberry brambles cover the forest floor.

Before my fae puberty, I couldn't see in the low light nor smell all the varieties of flora. Not what I had expected being a middle-aged woman to be like, but the changes are not all good. I don't mind wrinkles or having a bit more padding on my hips and thighs, but my new antlers get tangled in branches more than once, and it's as embarrassing as it is unpleasant.

"Good thing we weren't trying to be stealthy," Princess says, but there's gentle ribbing, not meanness in her tone.

I've known her long enough and experienced both to know the difference. Afraid I was using Gabriel for some nefarious purpose; she challenged me the first time we met.

Despite the growing tightness in my chest over Gabriel's disappearance, I smirk. "You grow antlers in a matter of months and try your prowling skills."

Princess scoffs. "No thanks. Shifting into a giant honey badger fills my quota of weird for a lifetime."

I chortle, freeing others to do so. We all exist in a society not setup for who we are and what we look like. I'd hoped coming out would change that.

A gentle touch on my arm grabs my attention. Phyr is at my side. He says in High Fae, "Change is often painful and filled with setbacks and heartbreaks, but in the end, change for better is worth the toil."

We head off the trail, navigating through ferns, pausing to disentangle ourselves from the stray blackberry vine here and there. Eventually, we come upon a small clearing.

Princess points to a moss-covered boulder jutting from the side of a hill. "Here's where I found the cubs. They were on top, whimpering and huddled together."

Phyr touches the ground nearby. "There was a disturbance in the fabric of the universe here. A primitive sort of portal open and closed."

Witchcraft or something else, I wonder to myself. Witch portals are precise and have traveled through spellwork, likely as long as the fae have planes walked. The spell could be the work of some other sort of supe. I don't want to discredit shifter noses, but it seems unlikely a witch from my old coven or a coven elder would do a sloppy grab.

"How did they know exactly where he would step?" Princess asks.

Good question. I dip into my faelight, accessing my second sight, which allows me to see the color of magic.

I gasp at what I see and then shout, "Don't move!"

CHAPTER
NINE

Scattered in the near distance, about a dozen rectangular shapes glow faintly the white of witchlight. The magical illumination is so faint, I doubt shifters would have scented the magic buried under the leaves and topsoil until it was too late. Much like I hadn't sensed a letter in my mailbox because I hadn't expected it.

Planeswalkers aren't the only supes who can cross the interstitial space of the multiverse. Angels, Fallen, demons, and witches practice spellwork to create portals between places. I've banished hellhounds and left Gehenna that way.

"There are traps buried all over, at least a dozen."

"Why didn't anyone trigger them, but Gabriel?" Princess asked.

"Spells are usually coded with a specific person or intention in mind," Daystar replies, his Kairskan accent coloring his words.

"They meant to snatch Gabriel," I agree, blood heating as fury courses through me. Blood. Spells coded for a specific person, or a specific intention only work if you have the blood, nails, or hair. Even family members can succumb to the spell.

I twirl to Phyr. "Get Roxy!"

He nods, slicing through the air and disappearing. The fae prince reappears with a snarling and confused white wolf in his arms.

"Roxy, I told Phyr to get you. There's a harmful spell out here that may be directed at you. Be still."

The wolf stops moving and cocks her head, interested, and panting.

Phyr rolls his eyes and mutters something about high-strung children in High Fae.

Roxy, having the gift of the Herald, understands him and growls.

I turn to Princess. "Anyone else blood-related to Gabriel?"

"I'm his distant cousin through our mothers," Princess admits, grimacing. "Many of us are distant cousins."

I chew my lip, wondering why they shift into different animals. Packs of different animal forms made sense, if they were familial. Shifters are secretive about these things, so I let it go.

"Since we don't know which bloodline might or might not be affected, can you do the alpha call thing on all of them to the house?"

Princess pulls a face. "Alpha-call thing?"

"You know, when you go awooo!" Rhiannon mimics, a wolf howling at a moon.

"Ah, the alpha awooo," Princess replies, turning her smirk to me. "You should have made that clear."

I give her an apologetic look. It is insensitive, but Rhiannon means no harm.

Princess shrugs it off and nods to Roxy. "Would you do the alpha awooo for us when we return to the house?"

Roxy's wolf snuffs but releases a howl when we return to the house.

After the pack shifts into their human forms and get some clothes on, I address the group. "The woods aren't safe until I can neutralize the traps the witches have set up."

"You're absolutely sure it's witches behind this," Leilani asks, sidling next to her fiancé, Cian.

"The color of magic doesn't lie," I sigh. "I think the elders of my former witch coven are after me."

"How do we know that it's not his mother's coven again?" Aurora says, nodding toward Daystar.

She has good reason to distrust the Baba Yaga coven. They harmed her and tried to trap me into becoming part of their coven. However, I haven't had problems with them since that initial altercation.

Daystar holds up his hands. "I am not my family's keeper, but matushka enjoys Miriam's visits too much to cause trouble."

"It's true. I'm close with Ezmal and that coven is the council's ally."

Rhiannon, Jada, and I have made it up to Snoqualmie Pass once a month, to perform certain rites sacred to witches with the Baba Yaga coven. For the summer solstice last year, Ezmal and I invited all the covenless to celebrate with the coven.

"How do we confront these witch elders?" Princess asks.

"If we confront them, we're looking at a battle that we might not win."

"So, we just leave my dad with them?" Roxy's blue eyes are wide with disbelief.

I shake my head. "I'm going to go to my coven and offer myself in exchange for Gabriel."

"Mami, no!" Jada cries out. "They'll kill you."

"Dad wouldn't want you to do it," Roxy says. "We should fight."

Princess also chimes in, "The pack is behind a rescue attempt. They took our alpha. We can't let them take his mate in exchange for his life. It will weaken our position."

"You're not trading yourself for another council member," Lucinda agrees. "The entire territory will be compromised without your presence."

Leilani clears her throat. "As your co-council members and friends, Cian and I won't let you do it, Miriam."

Cian murmurs his agreement, his gaze shifting to Phyr.

"Not to mention what the High King would do if Gracia harmed you," Phyr adds.

There is that. Oberon wouldn't take any murdering of his child lightly. Given what my mother already cost him, in slights and family, this might be enough to push him to a war the fae can't afford.

Aurora remains quiet, her gaze on the house. She and Princess are parents now. The pack would take care of the cubs, but the poor dears already lost their biological mother. Plus, Aurora is a do no harm type of vegetarian. It would go against her values to fight.

"I wouldn't be upset if you stayed with your children, and I'm sure Gabriel wouldn't either," I say, hoping I'm right about his sense of family.

The bigfoot casts me a grateful smile.

"Why don't you have matushka negotiate for you?" Daystar offers.

"Thanks, but it's better if I negotiate with the Archivists myself."

"Intermediaries were often used in the old world to settle disputes between covens," he insists, "and mama is the most respected of all witches."

Rhiannon beams at her beau and then waggles her eyebrows at me. "Wouldn't hurt to show you have the most powerful witch on Earth as an ally."

Daystar places a hand on her shoulder. "The coven, especially matushka, would have to remain neutral, radnayia."

Getting Ezmal to agree would be fine, but the old witch's youngest sister still isn't keen on me for destroying the grimoires.

Lucinda nods as if deciding something. "I say diplomacy first and if that doesn't work—"

"We go in with talons and fangs," Princess finishes.

TEN

Like most covens, the Baba Yaga are wary of outsiders, so it's decided only Princess, Phyr, and I need to go with Daystar and Rhiannon to speak to the coven. The pack mobilizes to take the rest of the council home. The emergency is over and planeswalking takes a lot of Phyr's energy to do, but we need him fresh in case there's a fight in store for us later.

The girls go to the house. While I do this, knowing Jada remains under the protection of the shifters gives me some peace of mind.

Still, we haven't left yet because Princess and Aurora stand off to the side, arguing softly. My fae hearing lets me eavesdrop, whether I want to or not. It seems Aurora doesn't want her mate anywhere near the coven.

Phyr sidles next to me. "I have a plan."

I turn to face him. "I'm all ears."

The fae frowns at the American expression but saves commentary. I'm positive he'll look it up on his phone later and assimilate the phrase like a native speaker with a fae lilt.

"While you take a motorized vehicle to their property, I shall use a bit of Gabriel's hair to search for him while your former coven is distracted by this negotiation."

It's a good plan.

A splendid plan, actually.

Yet, my heart seizes at the thought of Phyr facing the Archivists alone. I know he can fend for himself, but if they have powerful enough spellwork to hold an archangel...

Phyr clasps my shoulders and presses his forehead to mine. "Speak your worries out loud."

My throat tightens. "I don't want you to go without me. It's too risky."

It's cowardly and selfish, and not the right thing to say at all, but having Gabriel gone missing hurts enough. I can't lose Phyr again. The witches took me from him, separating us for decades. Now that my closest friend is back in my life, I can't let them separate us again.

A grin tics at the corner of his mouth—one I don't need to be a mind reader to understand.

"Let's say I create an invisibility spell and promise only to see after his condition. Would that ease your worry?"

My heart lurches in my chest. I've only considered Gabriel kidnapped, not dead or worse.

"No. Not at all," I sigh. "Please, let me try to negotiate first and then we'll go together."

"Then it is decided." He backs away, sketching a slight bow.

He's done this before, asking permission for something and bowing at my reply. At one time, I believed it was a quirk of his. Now I know the reason.

Something occurs to me. "You know, I love that you confer with me before doing something dangerous, but you can do things without my permission." I certainly don't ask him for any.

"I can," he smirks, "but I won't."

My brows furrow together. "Why not?"

He presses a thumb between my eyebrows, as if pressing away

my worry. "Ah, this democratic society makes you forget your Unseelie hierarchies—you outrank me, my dearest friend."

Fae rulers aren't like human monarchs, taxing for riches. They are the lifeblood of their faerie, sacrificing their own faelight to sustain it. It's a symbiotic relationship of sorts. The fae ruler's power grows because those who inhabit and are nourished by the faerie believe in them.

"Phyr, I want you to be your own person," I insist. "We're not in the Unseelie Court. I'm not better than you are here."

Admiration fills his amber eyes. "That is why I'd follow you anywhere and do anything for you. You don't want to rule anyone, but you bear all the responsibility of a fae queen."

"You two ready?" Princess asks, arms folded across her chest. Aurora stomps her way back to the house in the background.

I nod and we're on our way.

Snoqualmie Pass in the winter versus in the late springtime are two different places. Vibrant green grasses and lovely wildflowers cover the meadow where the Baba Yaga coven has their secret compound.

Magic brushes my skin as we're welcomed through protective wards.

The colorfully painted cottages resemble something out of a Russian fairytale—gorgeous in their detail and eerie in the fading evening light.

Witches, three in black and three in red hooded robes, greet us on the pathway to Ezmal's cottage, red signifying witch law enforcement and black signifying judgment. By greet, I mean they block the path ominously, faces shadowed by their hoods—*this should be fun.*

"What's up, witches!" Rhiannon shouts.

The witch known as Friza lowers her hood. She directs her gaze at me. "Your friend is no longer welcome here."

Rhiannon glowers. "Are you talking about me?"

Friza hisses at her. Hisses!

"This is going to go well," I mutter, rubbing my head. "We're here to—"

"It was my choice," Daystar cuts me off, putting himself bodily between Rhiannon and Friza.

Shirom lowers her hood. There's sadness in her eyes. "You aren't welcome here either, Daystar, not until your mother forgives you."

"I fell in love. There's nothing to forgive."

I glance at Daystar and Rhiannon. Rhiannon could cause an earthquake and kill us all. Right now, she doesn't look a drop vengeful or scared. Deep sadness that reflects Shirom's feelings fill the rock witch's big brown eyes. To leave a coven is a serious offense, but to leave a coven alive with no retribution means the Baba Yaga coven does things differently.

Shirom shakes her head. "You broke our laws by practicing spellwork. Be happy we have only abjured you as punishment."

"I've served this coven for centuries. I deserve to be more than a stud," Daystar replies, but he's already turning his back on his aunt.

"Not every warlock is tainted by the old world. You raised Daystar to be a good person. You should trust in that," Rhiannon says quietly, joining her partner. "See you back in the car, Miriam."

I give her an apologetic look. My stomach knots as they walk away. I don't like starting this conversation without sticking up for my friends.

"They're right, you know, but that's not why I'm here," I say. It's not enough, but it's something. "I need to see Ezmal."

Friza shakes her head. "You're no longer held in Ezmal's favor. Daystar was her favorite son, and you and your covenless friends corrupted him."

"The Archivists kidnapped the archangel. If she doesn't see me, all witches might face the wrath of Heaven."

Shirom gasps. "You could have opened with that! We assumed you were here to plead for Daystar."

CHAPTER
ELEVEN

Ezmal's cottage hasn't changed since the first time I came here, when she tried to lure me into joining her coven. The elderly witch looks tired as she listens, the kind of bone tired one gets when you've dealt with a wayward child for much too long—if all their troubles started with some bad parenting choices on your part. Daystar moving in with Rhiannon likely isn't what she'd hoped for when she used her son to seduce my friend to get to me.

In my opinion, Ezmal got exactly what she deserved for trying to trick me into joining their coven instead of befriending me in the first place. There was a time I would have considered joining for protection and community, but by the time they tried to lure me, I had found supernatural friends in my own community and from my past who filled that space. Ezmal has become someone I'd call friend, too. However, I will not join a coven that will not allow anyone assigned male at birth to practice witchcraft.

Princess and I are welcomed in. Phyr remains outside the cottage.

"This is very serious. We will have to use a very powerful spell that will astral project us for the meeting."

I've only used astral projection once before and don't care to again. It's too risky. Not all ghosts start out dead. Some ghosts are witches attempting astral projection who never make it back to their bodies.

"No need." I wave the idea off. "I could have Phyr take us there. He's a planeswalker."

The elderly witch casts a pointed look at me. "I'm aware. However, I don't believe it is the Archivists who did this."

"Why not?" Princess asks.

She snorts and waves a dismissive hand as if we're idiots for asking. "Amateur work and very sloppy if you ask me. The Archivists have all the knowledge of the old world, they know you're half fae, they know what you're capable of, and kidnapping an archangel is idiotic. This sounds like someone wants to dismantle your council by taking out the two most powerful members and then sending the rest on a wild goose chase."

My heart lurches and the first place my mind goes is to my siblings setting up this chaos. However, they couldn't care less about the Supernatural Council of the Pacific Northwest and wouldn't break treaty with the Angelic Anocracy. They also hate witches. No. It wasn't Maeve or Nix.

"Still, while all that may be true, I'd like to speak to the Archivist coven to rule out it wasn't them."

"I agree. However, stepping on another coven's land without permission is an act of aggression. I will act as mediator for you, if you astral project with me."

If anyone had asked how I would prefer to spend my evening, I would have said, "Cozying up on the sofa with Gabriel, with the teens on the floor and Phyr in the overstuffed chair, criticizing the Great British Bakeoff or some other competitive baking show."

I would not have said "sitting cross-legged and holding hands with the elder witch of the Baba Yaga coven."

Stars twinkle overhead. Candles circle us. Our foreheads are greased with a salve that stinks of manure and herbs.

The witches of the coven gather around the circle of candles. They hum in unison. We are about to travel the multiverse with our minds, the witches' voices will guide us back to our bodies.

Magic is as thick as the humidity in the air, a weighted presence.

A bowl before us contains my hair, Ezmal's hair, and a lock of my mother's. We're going to project wherever she is. Since I haven't seen my mother in twenty years, and I stole and *destroyed* her coven's most prized asset, I'm not sure Gracia will welcome me with open arms.

I close my eyes as I chant the words of the spell in tandem with Ezmal. My stomach knots but I focus on the words and intention.

The transition takes seconds. Ezmal and I hover side by side in the sitting room of my old compound. The room is empty, and the house is eerily quiet. We're ghosts to anyone who sees us. We can see and hear, and be seen and heard, but we can't manipulate our surroundings, so no ringing doorbells or knocking over pots to get attention.

"Hello?" I call.

"I do not like this. We should have appeared before your mother."

Ezmal's voice is tinny and distant, as if she's speaking through a tube.

We float around the entire first floor. Not a single witch. It's late on the east coast, so we check the bedrooms. Every dorm is empty.

"Do you believe they changed locations?" Ezmal asks.

I shake my head, or at least think I do. I can't feel this form. "No. They can't. The grimoire library is too big."

"We must go to this library. Do you know where it is?"

I pause before consenting. I had no problem with Gabriel and Phyr coming with me into the library archives, but Ezmal was another witch. Trusting witches when witches tried to trap me, and kidnapped Gabriel, suddenly seems like a bad idea.

"I can't take the grimoires," Ezmal grumbles, "I'm assuming the wards on the library are strong enough to withstand a siege."

We float outside. The farm is quiet. The animals are likely asleep in the barn so it's not surprising. I lead through the farmyard; aware something isn't right. Something ahead stops me from going forward. I don't want to see it. I want to turn around; pretend I never came.

Ezmal whispers something in Kairska. A prayer, I think.

Her projected body is tethered to mine, so I must go with her as she approaches the gruesome scene.

"A battle took place here. A great one."

The corpses of witches lie in evidence of that. If I had my body, I would have thrown up by now. A magical battle took place. An ugly one. These women fought, with their lives, with whatever force they came across.

"Were the Archivists at odds with any other coven?" Ezmal asks.

"No. We—I mean they kept to themselves."

Ezmal sees something which causes her to wail and curse. Her ghostly eyes are wild with fear. She shakes her transparent head, repeating in Kairska, "This is not possible. They are dead."

I regard the spot she fixates on. There's a symbol burnt into the ground as if someone used a giant brand: a circle around a pentacle, each triangle of the pentacle has a Kairskan glyph and an eye within the pentagram of the pentacle.

"The Shadow Keepers coven," Ezmal announces in Kairska, her voice weaker than before.

"Warlocks," I gasp, knowing the name.

"We must go. They won this fight, which means they have the Archivist's grimoires. We must prepare for a war."

I survey the battlefield. "Not yet. There's something I've got to see for myself."

Gratefully, I don't need to explain that I mean I want to see my mother.

Now that I know who they fought, it doesn't take long to find my mother, or what remains of her. She'd been one of many of the old ones who fell defending the grimoires. Bitter anger sweeps through my spectral form. Those books meant more to her than I ever did.

That would be a bitter pill for future me to swallow, but right now, I'm numb. Judging by the bodies' state, they'd died weeks ago. Hundreds of witches died and not a single person came to their aide. It's their fault. They isolated themselves from society, so society didn't feel the need to protect them or even come out to check on them.

I reach for my mother's withered hand. She's aged so much in the years of our estrangement. I can't cry. I don't have a body. I don't know if I would cry if I did. She took my father, my faerie, and most importantly my Phyr from me, so I could be a pawn in her game.

"I don't know if I was ever anything to you, but you'd always been everything to me. I will endeavor to pass along the things you taught me as a witch, but I will, in time, forget you as you made me forget my father."

Unlike these witches, Gabriel has a large community of shifters, nephilim, covenless fae, demigods, and cryptids who care about him. I think of Agents Tan and Roanhorse of the International Supernatural Enforcement Agency, aka I.S.E.A., and formerly known as the U.N.M.U. They might be interested in warlocks from another world going around killing witches and kidnapping archangels.

We can do nothing for the bodies in these forms. It's probably for the best since the I.S.E.A. will need evidence to prove I'm not just spouting nonsense.

We check the archives. It reeks of sulfur. Thousands of grimoires either stolen or destroyed. I begin to weaken and feel the distance from my body.

"Let's return."

Ezmal's specter nods mournfully. "There's nothing here for us."

My eyes snap open, back in my body. The circle is broken.

Ezmal needs assistance to get to her feet and can't hold herself up once they get her there. She goes limp in her sisters' arms.

My limbs are also jelly. Phyr lifts me from the circle, cradling me against his chest.

"Our king cannot have his revenge. His consort is dead." It's all I can manage to say before I lose consciousness.

TWELVE

It takes three precious days for me to function fully in my physical body again. Three days of useless bedrest. Phyr and Jada take turns feeding me and seeing to my needs. My cousin Niamh and her dragon stand guard while Phyr and Jada assist Princess and the shifters in their continued search. I doubt the warlocks have him. A nephil would mean nothing to warlocks of the old world.

The damned warlocks likely knew we astral projected. I know the consequences, but let my distress fog my judgment. I shouldn't have listened to Ezmal and instead used my advantage of having a fae planeswalker.

I mourn those days, not for my mother. She doesn't deserve my grief. I mourn for the witches who knew no other life. Those who served the coven faithfully and died protecting the last link to the old world.

When I can get on my feet and walk downstairs on my own, Rhiannon, Jada, and all the covenless in the territory gather at my house.

We caravan out to the woods where the Baba Yaga coven dwells.

It's a sunny day in the mid-sixties. The stench of death muddies the fresh mountain air.

Coven-bound and covenless witches gather around a stack of wood almost two stories high. Atop the stack is a platform, the funeral pyre with my mother's body. After documenting the crime scene, I.S.E.A. allowed Phyr to open a portal so the witches could transport the bodies here where they could be remembered, instead of that farm where they were believed to outsiders, as cultists.

In a way, they were. The witches isolated themselves, living in the past. My mother always said it was for our protection, but it did nothing but alienate witches from ever being part of this wonderful, chaotic world. They would have destroyed the inhabitants of this planet just to have what they once had somewhere else. It may be callous to think so, but they got what they deserved.

Jada and I, the remaining descendants of the Archivists, each carry a torch. We light the pyre. Tears stain Jada's cheeks. She's never seen so many dead before.

Truthfully, neither have I. But I'd already mourned their wasted lives and have no more tears left.

As the pyre burns down, we have a pagan feast celebrating their lives, and I tell stories of my coven. We witches sing songs in Kairska. Songs to mourn the passing of their light. We sing of rebirth, guiding their light to the next generation.

Before Jada and I leave, Ezmal takes me aside. The wizened witch clasps my hand. "Today we mourn. Tomorrow, we plan for war."

THIRTEEN

Phyr knocks on my bedroom door shortly after Jada and I return from the funeral.

"Enter," I call from my vanity as I apply lotion to my face. I just got out of the shower to wash the charnel stink from my hair and skin.

In the vanity mirror, I watch him sit on my bed; the mattress dipping under his weight. He rakes his fingers through his long, silky hair.

"I cannot fathom why the warlocks would want Gabriel, or any of the shifters on his property. The archangel has nothing to do with avenging their world."

He has a point.

"Who would benefit from me and Gabriel gone?" I ask, applying lotion to my neck and where the robe has exposed my chest.

"The angels and your siblings are the two most obvious choices. Nix and Maeve are against the fae returning to this world. However, while I was working, this came on the bakery television."

Phyr retrieves a cell phone from his pocket and brings it over to me, pulling up a video and pressing play.

A woman in her fifties wearing a dress jacket, high-collar shirt, and long floral skirt sits in an overstuffed chair. She's crying so hard I can't understand what she's saying. Not that I want to hear anything Mary Orwell, the wife of the pastor who ran the Paradise Centers, has to say.

Across from Mary sits a man in a tailored suit. He hands her a tissue. I recognize him as Pastor Ted Rios, a televangelist who has mega-churches throughout the North, Central, and South Americas. New churches are under construction in Africa, Australia, and Asia. All his churches televise his sermons. – Rios keeps himself central to his ministry, so most of the money not spent in funding more churches goes to his mega-mansion, stock of expensive cars, and four jumbo jets.

I know all of this because Jenna Jones had one of his former staff on her exposé show.

My chest tightens.

Ted Rios has nothing to do with the Paradise Center scandal. Besides accumulating wealth—and likely magic from his believers—he supposedly preaches acceptance of supernaturals as God's creatures. However, this woman is the wife of Pastor Orwell. She's supposed to be in jail.

"No modesty was allowed. I had to take care of bodily necessities and shower in front of other women—lesbians." She whispers "lesbians" as if saying the word would summon them, like saying "Lucifer" gains his notice.

Not the same thing, lady, not by a long shot.

I already don't like her for what her church did to supernaturals, but the implied perversion of lesbians for their sexual orientation is just icing on the loathing cake I have for Mary Orwell.

"Not that they aren't God's creatures—but the whole indecency of it all," she continues.

I pause the video. I can't watch anymore without losing my shit. It's been a hard week as it is. I glance over my shoulder at Phyr. "How is she out of prison?"

"A very good attorney got her acquitted. She divorced Pastor Orwell. Apparently some videos have surfaced of his infidelity."

A *lot* has surfaced about Orwell after our exposé on Jenna Jones. Not much has surfaced about his wife. She played the doe-eyed innocent during her trial, but she also admitted knowing about the holding cells in the Paradise Center basements.

"How could she possibly be acquitted?"

"She claims she saw documentation that her husband was running a drug detox center under the Paradise Centers and kept it quiet. The documentation showed up. It was all falsified, but her lawyer claims that's how her husband tricked her and that he made the forgeries."

"Did Orwell testify he lied to his wife?"

Phyr shakes his head. "No. But, his reputation is shot. I think the judge might be in Rios's pocket."

I smile at Phyr's usage of the modern expression despite the terrifying fresh development of Mary Orwell's release. "Why would Rios want to help Mary?"

"That video is about her repenting and accepting supernaturals as worthy of God's love. She claims God made angels and humans all different, so supernatural abilities might mean they're chosen ones of God, maybe even the original Israelites."

"Shit. That's a wild spin."

"Yeah. But it puts belief where they want it. Think about supes that want acceptance. If under Rio's guidance, Mary Orwell can change her attitude..."

The implications stagger the mind.

"What does any of this have to do with me and Gabriel?"

"Revenge? I did some research. Rios has supes in his congregations all over the world—" Phyr pauses, placing a comforting hand on my shoulder, "—including former witches and *sons* of witches. Their testimonials are pretty damning of covens."

"Revenge wouldn't serve their spiel that supes are chosen ones but getting us out of the way as a safe haven for witches and other supes is. Who better to blame than witches?"

Phyr smiles. "There's the fae princess raised in Oberon's court."

I send the video to Princess, along with my theories. I send a similar text to Agent Tan who works for I.S.E.A., or the International Supernatural Enforcement Agency, formerly known as the U.N.M.U. United Nations Monster Unit. The new name is a little more palatable, but the organization polices supes like me, or at least tries to. Within minutes, Tan responds with a text.

Tan: Interesting theory. Want to work as a liaison for the I.S.E.A.?

Me: What's involved?

Tan: Keep investigating Rios. If you end up in trouble, I'll back you as our liaison, looking into the welfare of supernaturals. Stay within your community.

After showing Tan's response to Phyr, I screenshot and forward the text to Princess. My phone rings seconds later. I don't need to put it on speaker for Phyr's sake—he has fae hearing, but I do anyway.

"You think Rios used witches to trap Gab—Don't nip your brother that hard or I'll collar you." A pup whines in the background. "Sorry. You think zealots are behind this?"

"Ezmal said it was piss poor work, and it's obviously not my old coven." The smell of the pyre and memories of all the slain witches wafts into my head.

"That would make more sense than warlocks taking Gabriel. They have nothing to do with anything."

Another text comes in from Tan.

"Hold on," I tell Princess, as I switch my screen to read messages.

Tan: A field agent just sent this from the Arlington office. The coven was based in the Monongahela National Forest, near the border of West Virginia. Twenty-five bodies.

I read the text a few times, grasping the meaning and letting the impact settle in.

The message has an attachment. I take a deep breath before opening it.

Pictures of another remote coven destroyed. This time, the house is burned to the ground. Same brand on the ground.

I rub my temple and blow out my breath.

Phyr squeezes my shoulder. "Miriam, are you well?"

"No. Twenty-five witches are dead. They had some interaction with the Archivists." As much as rival covens could. "I knew them."

His features show no reaction, no emotion, but I'm used to that from Phyr. "Where was the coven?"

"A forest on the border of Virginia and West Virginia."

"Sounds like the warlocks are moving south and west."

I text Agent Tan that there's another coven in West Virginia, due west of the besieged coven. I give her the approximate location, noting they might have switched locations in recent years.

Something else occurs to me.

"There is a coven in central Virginia and another in western Pennsylvania, who are not allied with the Archivists. They want nothing to do with Lucifer and they've gone unscathed so far."

"Better let the feds know. It'll build trust," Princess suggests. "Look, I got to get the pups ready for bed. The council should meet and plan what we're going to do about Rios tomorrow. I think this supe-accepting pastor is our best lead to finding Gabriel."

I do too and tell her so. After I hang up with Princess, I text Agent Tan the information about the covens and their affiliations.

Tan: I.S.E.A. will offer them protection. Could you forward me a map with the locations of all the covens you're aware of? We could post agents to prepare for these warlocks.

I show Phyr the text. "Should I?"

"I'm not sure if I am the best person to ask. I have no loyalty to witches unless they are under your care. The question is, do you trust I.S.E.A. with the information?"

I frown. Because she helped me expose the Paradise Centers and Reverend Orwell in the first place, I trust Agent Tan, and to some degree, her partner, Agent Roanhorse, but the entire global organization? The United Nations Monster Unit, emphasis on the monster, was formed to police supernaturals, not protect them. A name change only after supes come out is for optics not progress.

I text Agent Tan that it will take some time to give her all the locations, but I give her a few more locations of covens I know of in the meantime, in hopes the act of good faith serves the witches some protection.

FOURTEEN

T he Supernatural Council of the Pacific Northwest gathers on colorful, overstuffed furniture in Lucinda's cafe. The others sip refreshments and talk about their lives. We haven't officially begun yet. We expect guests.

I stand by the door, waiting for the Baba Yaga sisters to arrive.

The three appear seemingly out of nowhere. Surprisingly, all three are in somewhat modern dress. Ezmal could be a babushka ripped from a cover of National Geographic, with her scarf-covered hair, shawl, sweater and long skirt. Friza wears fashionable slacks and blouse with expensive looking sunglasses. Shirom has on a summer dress. Each of them lends an arm to the elderly witch.

I welcome them inside and Lucinda gets them settled. The three witches take a seat in comfy chairs. Lucinda brings throw pillows for the elderly Ezmal for support. Then she offers all three refreshments. There's a reason Lucinda and I have been such close friends for so long. We both see to the needs of our community.

Aurora glares at the witches, no doubt still feeling prickly after they'd wounded her a year ago. She's agreed to set aside her differences with the coven for this meeting. I hope she can stick to it and not go Chewbacca on us.

Ezmal nods at Cian when I introduce him.

To her sister, she says in Kairska, "A luck worker. Very good for us." Her expression darkens with her sigh. "We will need it."

Phyr appears with my father and my two siblings. I cock my head questioningly at Phyr as Lucinda once again rises and welcomes the newcomers inside.

Maeve and Nix accompany Oberon, whom Lucinda leads to a high-back chair. We discussed the seating arrangement before the meeting, and we agreed this would be the only chair my father wouldn't begrudge setting his high fae backside upon.

"Why are my siblings here?" I whisper to Phyr.

He grimaces. "They won't allow a warlock the satisfaction of killing you when it should be their right."

"Comforting," I grumble.

Phyr smirks, but only shortly as he takes a position behind me.

I introduce my father to the witches.

The doorbell rings as Shawn comes through late. "Sorry. Traffic was—" The seraph's eye narrow on Nix.

My sibling grins, dark eyes lighting with amusement.

Shawn does not have the power to smite. He's defenseless against fae.

"This is a neutral space. Safe for all allies," Leilani reminds everyone.

My father's gaze turns to the demigoddess. I try not to gag at the appreciative once over he gives my friend. Now that I have my memory back, I know that the rose petal gown Oberon made Leilani was no small gift. Among fae, the act would be a gesture of courtship towards making her his consort.

I'm not the only one who dislikes Oberon eyeing Leilani. Poor Cian shifts uncomfortably.

Not noticing the discomfort he's causing me and Cian, my father smiles at Leilani. "Indeed, lovely one, my presence here is solely to offer the aid of my armies if need arises." He presses his hand to his heart. Woe and grief touching his features—not enough to mar his handsome face, but enough for effect. "These warlocks murdered my late consort in cold blood. Wayward as she may have been, their actions call for retribution. Not only have they offended me in this manner, but they also present a threat to my heir." His gaze sweeps to Shawn. The bereavement and flirting disappear, and he is once more the regal high fae. "Anyone who acts as my daughter's ally against these villains shall not worry about retribution for all previous acts of war from me."

"Shall we begin?" Shawn asks.

Lucinda squeezes my hand as I tell the council, my family, and the Baba Yaga sisters about what happened to my former coven and the coven on the border of West Virginia.

I'm dry eyed when I say the grimoire library is gone. Surprisingly so. Those grimoires have been my ancestors' task for millennia. In the end, preserving the grimoires didn't save them from the mistakes of the past.

I then relay something only Phyr, Princess, and I know. I tell them about Pastor Ted Rios and Mary Orwell's release from prison and the potential that they've used witches to do their dirty work.

"Witches have sided with zealots?" Ezmal shakes her head.

"This happens when a witch is raised without a coven," Friza says in English so everyone can hear. Expression dour, she shakes her head. "They don't know the price we've paid for allowing greedy men to rule us."

"You're right. Witches need guidance and protection of a coven, so they're not used for their powers at anyone's whim," Agent Tan says from behind me. She and Agent Roanhorse must have come in while I detailed the situation.

I'd invited them, so it's not a complete surprise, but Agent Tan couldn't commit to showing up.

"It also makes you xenophobic and not willing to work with authorities," I disagree, then introduce the agents. "This is Agent Tan and Agent Roanhorse of the International Supernatural Enforcement Agency."

Agent Tan holds up her hands. "We're not here in an official capacity. I would have to recognize this council as a legal entity if we were."

Roanhorse's gaze narrows on my fae family. "And make sure all guests in attendance are in the United States legally." He doesn't concentrate on Oberon, but on Maeve and Nix, "and not breaking any inter-world trade treaties. Again."

"We're all close family of a U.S. citizen," Maeve replies coolly, indicating my father and Nix in the "we" before gesturing to me, the U.S. Citizen. My sibling, pushing the truth and omitting the whole story, in true fae fashion. "No interworld trade is broken on our visit to our dear sister."

Shawn shifts uncomfortably in his chair. He came out to the world as an angel, not a U.S. born citizen. I wonder, as a supe lawyer, if he knows about interworld laws.

Perhaps because Tan and Roanhorse assume I was born here, or had bigger fish, like Pastor Orwell and a homicidal shifter, to fry when I met them. I wonder if my birthplace might come up later.

Tan places a gray tile about the size of a cup coaster on a table. "Lights, please."

Once Lucinda gets the lights, a realistic hologram projects from the tile. First, we see images of churches the size of a warehouse, then jets, and then multiple properties.

"Ted Rios has built his ministry on the recovery of former addicts, the homeless, ex-cons, and ex-military—who saw or did things they can't forget," Agent Tan begins. "He preaches salvation and forgiveness, showing the transformations of the recovered. These transformations attract people who have committed what he calls 'the little big sinners.'"

It makes sense. *If that person could be washed clean, so can my online gambling addiction or habitual cheating.*

"Not only does he save the soul, he saves the person. Rios

ministries has lots of resources to turn someone's life around besides the Sunday sermon," Roanhorse adds. "The homeless get jobs and homes. Sick parishioners who can't afford insurance receive health-care. The lonely find family and community."

It sounds good from the outside, but I don't like the dependency on the organization. My fae blood senses the debt and a price to be paid for this charity.

We watch a small clip of a person give a testimonial on how multiple doctors said that she would never walk again. Then a revival where Pastor Rios lays hands on the person from the testimo-nial. She gets up from her wheelchair and walks.

I've seen this sort of thing before. The person was never disabled. However, in the fakes, they walk unsteadily and then grad-ually get as sure as they've been walking their entire life. This, however, is like watching a newborn foal staggering about. Her brain hasn't caught up with the new ability yet. Embarrassment colors her features—almost as if she wants to do a better job of walking.

"I've seen her medical records. It's the real deal," Agent Tan confirms.

Agent Roanhorse hands Princess a thumb drive. "This has the blueprint of the probable location of where your alpha is being held, a full roster of Rio's security team at that location, and where they're stationed and patrol." Tan doesn't let go right away, giving the interim alpha a pointed look. "You didn't get this from me."

"Get what from who? Don't know what you're talking about." Princess smirks and stuffs the thumb drive into her pocket.

"That's all we can do for you regarding that," Agent Tan says, switching the hologram to reveal the gruesome scene of my former coven's farm. Then, she shows the aftermath of the other coven's property, and then a third coven I didn't know about.

"Our experts tested the wards around all three coven properties. Strong blood magic. It took days for the I.S.E.A. mages to break the wards on the second and third compound, but they noted the wards had not been compromised before they entered the crime scene of each compound."

I exchange looks with Lucinda. Judging from her wide-eyes, Lucinda also didn't know that the I.S.E.A. employed mages.

Mages are human practitioners of magic descended from druids or sorcerers of this world. From my coven's teachings, I erstwhile believed there were none left after the Fae Wars. Tan also led me to believe there were no supernaturals in I.S.E.A. I wonder if this is a recent development with the name change.

Agent Tan continues, "Given the readings our mages detected on the property, they believe the warlocks entered both communes within the protective wards. Which makes us question whether they had an insider witch?"

"Or, a disgruntled warlock," Agent Roanhorse adds, glancing at the Baba Yaga sisters.

"It's best to check in with your witches. Make sure everyone understands these warlocks leave no one unscathed. Helping them is in nobody's best interest," Agent Tan suggests. "What can you tell us about this warlock coven, unofficially, that could help our mages pursue them?"

Ezmal replies in Kairska in a low, trembling voice. Friza clears her throat and then translates, "I fear this is the end for me. What could your mages, with their spells so weak they take days to break protection wards, do? Nothing. It is best you turn your backs on this. You cannot fight them no more than an infant with a rattle could fight a seasoned warrior."

"I disagree," my father says. "The High Fae will assist any mages of druid ancestry in spellwork to defensive magics against warlock attacks."

"King Oberon," Shirom warns in a shaky voice. "The fae should stay safe in their faeries and not return to a world under siege by war gods. If my sister fears them, so should you."

"War gods sit among you," Oberon flicks his wrist at Leilani and then at me, before gesturing to himself and my siblings. "Humans worshiped our kind long before witches fled to this world. Druids sought us to amplify their own magics. Why do you think Gracia sought me for a single child to power a spell it took many of your witches to control?"

"I'd have to ask my superiors for the clearance for fae of another world to assist our mages," Agent Tan gives the hologram a mournful look. "I don't think I will have a problem. If history tells us anything, this won't stop at witches."

Maeve and Nix smile. They don't want any part of this world, but they do like me expendable. My chest tightens and I exchange a glance with Phyr. Oberon found a way in for the fae without me or Gabriel.

If my life wasn't forfeit before, it will be now.

Their smiles fade as Agent Tan amends, "Since Miriam is the High Fae resident of this territory, she will be the liaison for all incoming fae. She will have a large part in accepting who stays and who goes."

FIFTEEN

Agent Tan and Agent Roanhorse leave, first passing their cards to each of the council members and one to my father, which he immediately declines, "My daughter will be our means of communication."

Not missing a beat, Tan hands the one she would have given my father to Ezmal.

"What is this?" Friza asks for her sister.

"How to contact me. You might want us to help you with defense strategies."

Ezmal holds the piece of paper and makes a slight gesture that the agents wouldn't know. I know. She's clearing the card of tracking spells and/or ill will.

"We don't own a telephone," Friza informs, taking the card from Ezmal and placing it within her robes.

Agent Tan grins and nods, as if expecting the statement. "There are instructions on the back to reach a druid on my team through other means."

Friza narrows her eyes. "We don't work strange spells. We will contact Miriam."

Fun. I'm the supernatural telephone operator.

"Well, that's all from us," Agent Tan says with a slight nod to everyone.

With no goodbye, Agent Roanhorse opens the door.

"Miriam," Agent Tan says, gesturing for me to follow. "A moment, please."

She watches Roanhorse get in a sleek black vehicle before turning to me. "You need to claim your territory and align it with your faerie."

I furrow my eyebrows. "What do you mean?"

"The mages say that in the olden days, before what they call The Great War, powerful high fae made themselves a part of the flora and fauna where they lived. The people who live on that land become people they protect or punish for wrongdoing."

"I don't know." I really don't. Tethering myself and my faerie to this world doesn't seem right. There will be something I need to give up. I don't want to become a being that wanders the cosmos, but I also don't know what tying my light to the land will do.

"According to our mages, claiming the land will make it harder for the warlocks—or anything else—to fight you." She emphasizes anything else. With Rios gaining followers, so does the Angelic Anocracy. A power boost right when they're about to go after Gabriel isn't good.

"I'll have to learn more about the process."

"I'll have the Archmage contact you." She hands me a card with the name Gavin Doyle. "Doyle is from an ancient line of druids, supposedly with fae blood himself. He'll be the one coordinating any efforts between his department and your kith and kin. He's the one who needed the coven locations."

I don't commit to anything and simply nod instead of thanking Tan. I pocket the card in my leggings as I watch her join Agent Roanhorse in an unmarked vehicle.

When I return inside, Shawn has the floor. "I'll put out feelers on whether the Angelic Anocracy knows of Gabriel's kidnapping. I can't believe that Pastor Rios is acting alone. There might be a seraph involved, if not another archangel."

"Your former brethren are less direct than when I last encountered them," Oberon notes.

"The angels have always dealt with humans indirectly," Shawn disagrees. "It's part of the Angelic Code. All glory must go to the Creator. In their eyes, Gabriel has taken some power for himself. They are using this pastor to show he isn't a god."

"They want the power and control, but fear the leash of a godhood," Maeve remarks.

"I don't blame the angels. I don't want to be a god, serving humans either," Nix adds in High Fae. "The druids betrayed us once. That's enough for me."

Oberon's face darkens, but only briefly. Anyone who isn't fae doesn't understand that Nix directly denounced our father's ambitions. The High King regards my sibling with an amicable expression and conversational tone. "We will discuss your involvement in your sister's defense when we are out of mixed company."

"If they don't wish to aid me, I do not mind if they stay out of the fight," I say in High fae. I would rather not have my siblings working with mages of druid ancestry, or anyone in this world at all.

Gabriel wouldn't like any of it.

"As you wish, daughter." My father rises and nods to Phyr.

I kiss Oberon's cheek.

"Bind yourself to Phyr before they kill you and blame the warlocks," he whispers in High Fae, so faint I hardly hear it. He says in louder English, "I hope you find your lover. He's not like his brethren and if he's been taken, the Anocracy knows he may prove to be a challenge to them."

CHAPTER
SIXTEEN

With Rhiannon moved out and Jada at Roxy's, it's only Phyr and I pulling up to the dark house after the meeting. My stomach flutters, nerves over what I must ask him to do.

"What did the king whisper?" Phyr asks, relieving me of thinking how I would bring it up.

I lick my lips. "He said we need to bond soon."

Phyr is quiet for a moment. "The bond will fortify us against the coming tide."

It's about time I accept the bond so that we can be stronger together, especially if more fae are coming.

"I agree." I kiss the corner of Phyr's mouth.

He's very still. I don't think he even breathes.

I open my car door to get out.

His hand grips my wrist, pulling me gently back into my seat. "I have a friend. A fae named Oisin. He is powerful and would cherish bonding solely to serve you."

I remember Oisin from my scattered childhood memories. A warrior fae, ancient and powerful, he had frightened me as a small child. I remember no fond looks or kind treatment from the warrior as I grew older. I remember him sparring with my cousin and having quite a distinct look in his eyes and tone when he spoke to them.

"I had thought he'd bond with Niamh."

Phyr shakes his head. "He's promised himself to be your consort upon maturity." He gives me an apologetic look. "Once we had a child."

I furrow my brow. I distinctly remember choosing Phyr as my consort, but never Oisin. "I don't remember this."

"It's tradition that several fae of varying lower courts promise themselves to serve the monarch and the heir. Oisin is Niamh's lover, but he was one of many chosen to serve the heir as consort at your birth. It's fae tradition to have at least ten lined up." He grins as if remembering something fondly. "It caused quite a scandal that you chose me, not even a firstborn of my house as the one who would serve as your—"

I put my hand up. "Blessed Danu's tits, if you're going to say stud, or anything of the like, I will absolutely vomit."

Phyr laughs. "I want to let you know that if you want me nothing more than your consort in name, there are others who wouldn't mind carrying on their lives without your love, but as your servant. They would die for you, Miriam."

"Because I'm Oberon's daughter?" Funny how dear old dad didn't mention any of this.

"Because you're the heir. If you take the throne, your light is the source of *everything*. The high fae will cease to exist without an heir strong enough to take Oberon's place."

"You want my love?"

"I've said as much. If you don't reciprocate my romantic feelings, I want you to know I won't ask you to release me from my duty without a willing and even more powerful fae to take my place."

How I love Phyr differs from the way I love Gabriel. The way I love Gabriel is bright and hot, and sometimes a bit consuming. There is also a gentler side to our love. We are excellent protectors and parents. I owe it to Gabriel to not only become part of the supe community, but a leader. He helped me believe in myself again, to face Lucifer and stop running.

The way I love Phyr is the way you love the best parts of yourself. Phyr is my confidante, my companion, my partner in all things mundane, and stepfather to Jada. He is the tie to my magical child-hood and my gateway to the future. I am attracted to Phyr in the swoony way a young woman moons over their first love. As a grown woman, I'm aware of the way he moves, and the way he treats me bodes well for the way he'll behave as a lover.

"All my relationships have failed. I'm afraid that if we cross the line between friendship and lovers, that it will break us," I admit. "Losing you would hurt worse than anything I've ever lost. If I lose you, I'll lose myself."

Phyr leans across the console of the car, cupping my face tenderly. He kisses me slow and tender.

I return the kiss with the same languid ardor, receiving the slide of his tongue. I reciprocate, careful to avoid his fangs the way he's careful of mine.

Since our reunion, we'd kissed once. I had gone through the worst night I'd had since I left Hell. Gabriel had seemed to act against me. My whole soul ached. With a kiss, Phyr filled every crack, strengthened every point so bent I'd almost broken. This kiss, though, is not a fae bolstering the Heir. He places all the long-bridled passion and the love he feels for me in this kiss.

Somehow, we disentangle and make our way into the house, stopping to kiss and touch.

I haven't seen him act shy since we were very young. Suddenly, I have my own case of shyness. I know he's not inexperienced like when we were young, playing Consort and Queen. Neither am I, but I feel my face flush and I have a moment of insecurity. Fae tend to be lithe and ethereal in their beauty. I'd gained some fae attrib-utes since my second puberty, but I have the fluff of a middle-aged mom, maybe a little extra than fluff. Gabriel likes me thick, but fae

—an image of Fand and their dancer's body comes to mind unbidden.

"Are you having doubts?" Phyr asks, misconstruing my pause.

"I'm half witch. I've had a kid. I'm not," I blow out my breath, embarrassed I'm admitting this insecurity, "all sinew and muscle."

A wicked grin curves Phyr's pretty mouth. His hand drifts over my waist, squeezing the fleshy part of my hip. "I know."

My phone plays "Best Friend" by Megan Thee Stallion and Sweetie.

Phyr chuckles and quirks a dark eyebrow. "Best friend?"

"It was funny at the time," I reply, and then pull out my phone from my purse to answer. "Hey, Princess."

"We're retrieving him tonight. You and Phyr in?"

I take a moment to process. I don't know what retrieving Gabriel would entail if we're going to do it at night. Princess and I failed at a rescue attempt almost a year ago. Turns out mortal weapons can work on supes. The True Believers tased me repeatedly. That isn't an experience one soon forgets. Also, I don't understand why Princess wants to go with so little preparation. The facility likely has armed guards.

While I deliberate, Phyr takes the phone from my hand. "Yes. We're in."

"Alright, come to the house in an hour." Without waiting for my reply, Princess disconnects.

"I suppose this changes our plans." I can't help feel the sting of disappointment, yet at the same time, the urgency to rescue Gabriel builds within me.

He cups my cheek. "My dearest, I'm a planeswalker. We could spend years together in faerie and return to this very moment."

"My mind can accept that. If only my heart could understand and not feel guilty. I would be furious if Gabriel knew I had been kidnapped and galivanted off on a twenty-year side-quest like a band of hobbits, elves, and wizards."

Phyr's brows quirk, as they usually do when I refer to something about Earth culture he yet hasn't caught up on.

He slides his hand down my arm and grasps mine. "I've waited much longer than twenty years for our reunion. I can wait a little longer."

CHAPTER
SEVENTEEN

Five minutes after Princess calls, Jada and Roxy show up to retrieve rescue-appropriate clothes for Jada. The two teenagers rumble down the stairs like stampeding elephants, not two women in their late teens. They're dressed in sweats and t-shirts, loose clothes they don't care about to shift into their animal forms. It's half-past eleven.

After what happened to her with the Paradise Center zealots, I don't want Jada to come, but she's almost nineteen, which means I don't get to call the shots about what she does and doesn't do anymore.

My mother never gave me any choice. Gracia took me from my fae kin and threw me into the fires of Hell as a weapon for Lucifer to use. My life was never mine in her eyes. For that, she died without ever knowing her granddaughter.

A tear escapes, sliding down my cheek, warm and wet. I wipe it away. There's no point in crying over a woman who never cared about me. I shutter out a thousand memories that say different. All it takes is one act of gross betrayal to do the unforgivable.

Phyr waits for me at the bottom of the stairs. He slides an arm around my shoulder. "Can we confer for a moment while the younglings put their shoes on?"

Roxy and Jada snicker and make quips about "the younglings" while he whisks me from the foyer and down the hall to the kitchen.

Once we are in the kitchen, he hands me a to-go mug of coffee. "Speak your troubles, my dearest."

I take a sip, enjoying the calming effect of the taste and delaying my response. I can't lose it now. We're going to rescue Gabriel. "The shitty thing about Gracia dying is that I never get to confront her."

Phyr considers what I said, then asks, "What would confronting her resolve?"

It's my turn to consider. Would it change anything if we talked about the past? Would she be able to provide a reason for her actions that would make me forgive her?

"Closure. I'd get to tell her how I feel. I don't know why, but I think that'd help me move on."

Phyr takes my hand. "I can take you to her."

He could take me to Raf, too. Now or in the past. The multiverse is open to the planeswalker.

I reconsider his original question. Would confronting her resolve any issues, or would it open new wounds left to never be resolved? A thought occurs.

"We could warn her and the other covens about the warlocks."

Phyr shakes his head slowly, shoulders slumped and amber eyes haunted. "We cannot erase the scar that many deaths left. The multiverse will try to correct itself and that is not a thing you want."

He would know. The fae almost wiped themselves from existence, playing with planeswalking to fight an unwinnable war.

There will be no reconciliation with my mother, no saving her, only what is. "Our issues died with her, and I just have to accept that and move on." I squeeze the hand that's holding mine and kiss his cheek. "Time to focus on the living."

"Yes, anam cara." He smiles all the way to his eyes.

We join Jada and Roxy in the foray. Gabriel's daughter has a distraught look as she says, "What if they're wrong and the Anocracy has him?"

I open my arms and embrace her. "We're going to get your dad, no matter where he is."

Roxy wipes away a stray tear with her sleeve and nods, but I don't think she believes me. She can't feel the magic sinking through my skin into my bones, binding me to fulfill my promise.

Beyond Roxy, Jada exchanges a worried glance with Phyr. They know the cost of a promise Danu extracts. I will be bound for the rest of my life to search for Gabriel until he is found. I know this, but I've lived so long with a hex on my memory of being fae that I sometimes forget what it is to be fae. The rules are stringent, and the price is high.

Phyr says, "Ready?"

After we all nod, he slices his hand through the fabric of the multiverse, cutting it with his faelight, making a bridge between the interstitial space of the multiverse to the driveway of the farmhouse.

The shifters are already outside and assembled. Princess approaches, handing Phyr a wad of dark hair obviously pulled from a brush. "Work your magic, planeswalker."

The fae's amber eyes sweep from the dark wad in his palm to me. "I will bring us to the building where he is purportedly kept, but I refuse to open a door to the unknown. All of this could be a trap for Miriam."

Princess throws up her hands. "Her ex-coven is dead."

My friend rears his head and scoffs, as if she's forgotten the obvious. "We still have the warlocks and the angels to consider."

The pack beta worries her lip and crosses her arms, deliberating. Finally, she must come to the same conclusion because she swears under her breath. "How long and how many people can you let pass?"

The fae shrugs. "I've held temporary bridges for armies of a size unfathomable to your mind for as long as my king demanded."

Syd, a grizzly shifter, whistles low. "Damn. You're scary powerful."

Phyr nods, but there's no pride in his reply. "I am."

"Bad ass, bro."

The shifter doesn't understand the significance of what Phyr said, but I do. My chest aches with the knowledge this is a painful memory for my friend, not a thing he is proud of.

The fae used to be innumerable. At my father's command, Phyr opened a portal and bridge that led countless fae to their deaths. The Tuatha de Danann are now reduced to tens of thousands. Who could be proud of that?

Phyr says nothing, shows none of these feelings. Fae of his station, or any station, cannot afford to display any sentiment against their king's decision.

"Well, if Syd's done kissing your ass, could you?" Princess makes a chopping motion, mimicking Phyr cutting through the fabric of reality.

The fae inclines his horned head and makes a door. Princess goes through. Shifters in teams of threes follow. I stay back, waiting to cross with Phyr.

Side by side, we enter. I'm getting better about passing through these bridges, letting the sensation of falling pass. It's easier with Phyr next to me, setting me aright.

He powers these passings the way my light powers my faerie, without me even being conscious of it. His hand is on the hilt of his sword. The amber of his irises, his visible tattoos, and his armor glow green with his faelight.

I don't need a weapon. I have a mental catalogue of protection spells, and ways of using my faelight taught to me by the King of the High Fae, a.k.a. my father, to defend myself against my siblings and feral fae who would love to devour my light. Knowing how to use my faelight defensively feels new, only recently recovered from memories my mother had hexed. However, sparring with Phyr has made me more adept at using it. I've been preparing to fight my siblings.

However, nothing I'd ever learned in my life prepared me for what was on the other side.

CHAPTER
EIGHTEEN

A deafening screech assaults my ears like jagged spikes drilling into my skull. Magic slams into me like three-hundred-pound linebacker throwing all his weight into a tackle. Pummeled, I stagger backward.

Suddenly, the onslaught stops.

Shield! Now! Phyr's voice screams inside my head.

I pull faelight from the cache within my body. With my second sight that allows me to see magic, I now perceive a field of green light encompassing Phyr and I. The solidity of it wavers under attack of golden angelic light.

Even knowing what we face, I can't panic now. I take precious seconds to create a protective bubble around myself with my light.

Phyr's shield shrinks to only encompass him.

The onslaught of the angelic power threatens my defenses. I don't know how long I can keep this up without revealing just how much power I truly have. A halfling witch is one thing. Oberon's heir and all the power my father imbued me with before birth is quite another.

The shifters lay face down on the floor in the center aisle of a church, covering their ears. They're the blue of shifter light. I scan them, searching for Jada. I spot her on the floor. She's fine, her godly powers will protect her from anything an angel can dish out, but my motherly instincts scream, "protect."

Ahead, an angel emanates a brilliant golden glow like an earth-bound star—I'm seeing their magic. In the creature's hand is a flaming sword. Eyes made of angelic light land on the two of us. The angel opens its mouth again. Magic, strong and old, beats against my faelight shield. I pull more and more of it out of a cache to defend myself from a full angel with Grace.

Abandoning the audio/visual assault on the shifters, Light Bright rushes me and Phyr.

The fae prince raises his glowing green sword, ready to battle.

Phyr will die to protect me.

I can't let that happen, but I don't know what to do other than die at his side, fighting the thing.

To make matters worse, Jada gets to her feet. She's glowing bright with magenta light. She's behind the angel, unseen.

I can't let her fight a full angel.

My faerie, I scream in my head at my friend as I turn around and run.

The angel pursues us. Heeding my order, Phyr opens a door through time and space just as the angel gains on us. Even with my protective barrier, I can feel the heat. The angel doesn't have time to realize what Phyr is doing before all three of us are in my faerie.

Jada is hot on our heels.

The flame of the angel's sword dies, and their eyes dim to a light shade of burnished gold without sclerae or pupils. The angel dances about much like Lucifer did, trying to work some spell to escape my faerie. I recognize the angel in subdued form as Pastor Rios, the evangelical from television. No wonder the good pastor could heal the sick.

"You hold no power here," I drawl in my best imitation of my father, bored at court. Meanwhile, my heart threatens to escape my ribcage by force.

The angel whirls on me. "I am the Archangel Mercedes. Release me, foul creature, or I will bring the wrath of Heaven upon your head!"

Phyr sheathes his sword and takes a stance next to Jada. "I believe this angel is either daft or hard of hearing."

"I know this is a mockery of creation." The angel waves their hands around. "An illusion, a pale imitation of what the one true God makes. It is blasphemous and obscene."

"There isn't one god, and you don't get to disrespect my mother." There's something ancient and powerful in my daughter's tone. Something that kept Lucifer from pestering me while Raf was alive.

The angel regards my daughter with an assessing look. "Abomination."

Jada scoffs, "Takes one to know one."

The angel rears their head, indignant. "Me, an abomination? You're the result of rutting creatures. I was perfectly crafted by the hand of—"

"Blah, blah, blah." Jada makes her hand talk. "Nobody cares about your absentee manufacturer."

The angel grips their sword and snarls, "Rescind that statement!"

"That's enough," I say, putting myself between the nineteen-year-old and the ancient baby. "I'll return you to Earth or allow you to return to Heaven if you will tell me the whereabouts of Gabriel Crowfoot."

"That's who you are!" The angel narrows their eyes and points their sword at me. "I make no bargain with Lucifer's whore."

One second, I'm several feet from the angel, and the next I'm a breathing the same air. I rip their sword from their hand and throw it into a cache. The few seconds I held the sword, its power pulsed through me—guess Lucifer wasn't the only one with a special creator-made weapon.

The angel strikes me flat-palmed in the chest and they scream in my face. The blow hurts and the scream is loud as heck, but just a scream and just a push. Judging by the seraph's face, they expect more to happen and are stunned when it does not.

Catching my breath, I say, "Did you just try to smite me?"

The angel stares at their hand, not responding.

I grab their robes. My voice is dangerous and low, as I ask, "Did you try to *smite* me?"

If they had, it would have killed Jada and Phyr, and any unsuspecting fae watching from behind the flora of my faerie.

The angel falls to their knees, weeping. "I have been forsaken."

"This angel must not have fought in the Great War," Phyr comments. "They should know smiting doesn't work in faeries."

"You are wrong, foul creature! The creator is all powerful." There's less heat in the second proclamation, as if their unwavering belief took a hit. "I have lost my Grace."

I roll my eyes. "You haven't. Those abilities don't work here."

Mercedes shakes their head woefully. "My God is omnipotent."

Jada snorts. "No god is omnipotent. Explain nasty stuff that happens to good people."

The angel glares at her but doesn't retort.

Jada rolls her eyes. "Uh-huh. Thought so."

Phyr agrees with my daughter. "Powerful, maybe. Omnipotent, he is not, not in the way you think, at least. Gods are not infallible. You'll love yours better when you see him as someone who means well but isn't perfect. A healthy dose of humility that you preach to the humans regarding your own powers might make you less of an ass, too."

"What are you going to do to me?" The angel has genuine fear in their eyes, realizing for the first time that I can end their existence.

"Tell me where Gabriel is, and I'll let you go." The magic of the promise settles into my bones.

The archangel wastes no time before answering, "The Seraphim Order stripped Gabriel of Grace. He disappeared before facing further punishment."

"Where did he go?"

Mercedes shrugs. "No one can find him. His father is not to blame."

I glance at Phyr, who has fewer scruples than I do. He dove into the angel's mind. My friend nods. It's the truth.

"Where do you want to go?" I ask.

The angel blinks, shock shaping their expression. "I haven't told you anything useful."

"You told me what you know, and that's good enough."

The dubious look lasts for a few moments. Likely eons of brain washing settles in. "I must go back to my territory. I was ordered to kill you, but I have decided it's the Lord's will to not do so. If you touched my sword and did not perish, you are not what the Angelic Anocracy believes you to be. "

"Before I take you back, do you want your sword?" I ask.

Phyr, Jada, and even the angel, look at me, perplexed.

"Mami. No. Don't give that asshole their sword back."

"Anam cara—" Phyr begins.

I hold up my hand, stopping Phyr from giving advice. *I have a plan;* I think at him.

The angel lowers their head. "I will not use the sword against you. Please, it was a gift from my creator before he left."

"I need you to promise me to never use it in vain and that the sword will only swing true if you are using it exactly as your creator intended."

Phyr still looks nervous in my periphery. Jada looks on with consternation in her features but doesn't interrupt. The angel deliberates, likely trying to suss out what I'm doing and if it's a trick. It is and isn't, but I will not return the sword without the intention made clear.

"I swear it."

I shake my head. "I want you to swear it on the sword itself."

The angel's mouth twists, but they agree.

I pull the sword out of the cache. Holding it is intense, this sword was made for an angel's hand not mine. However, I assume it might be the same for angels. Because, when I ask the angel to grip it with me, their expression changes.

I make the angel repeat the promise word for word.

"I promise not to harm this angel if they do no harm to those under my care."

Magic swirls around us, Danu and the angel's creator's magic, different in their nature despite being of two gods. My faelight and the angel's Grace light glow briefly as the oath settles in on us. I let go of the sword.

"You have bound me to my word?"

It's a rhetorical question. I answer it anyway, "As I am bound to mine."

"I would tell Archangel Gabriel about his son's mistress, but my brethren won't believe a halfling witch and once consort of Lucifer is as honorable as you are, let alone having good intentions."

"Lucifer has good intentions," I reply with a smile, "but poor means."

CHAPTER
NINETEEN

"He's been stripped of his angelic Grace," I say, choking on the words. Tears slide down my cheeks. I don't have to keep my emotions out of the news now that an angel isn't around.

The council is present, and we're all sitting around the table in my dining room. Shawn sits in the meeting in Gabriel's stead. Lance and Phyr lean against the counter rather than sit with the council.

"I figured that was the only way anyone could hold him for longer than a few hours." Princess sighs into a mug of coffee. "So, we're back to square one."

Leilani clutches her fiancé Cian's hand.

Lucinda casts a consoling look in my direction.

I know it's not my fault, but the guilt that this started because of me and the World Destroyer spell will not go away.

"He's without Grace and escaped," Shawn says, rubbing his hand over his short-cropped curls. "That's no small thing to go through. We have to consider that if he didn't come straight home, Gabriel might be hiding from us as well as the angels."

"Where did you go when you were stripped of your Grace?" Leilani asks.

It was on all of our minds, but I'm glad I wasn't the one to pry.

Shawn puffs out his breath. "This is something I've never shared. Lucifer personally came for me. I didn't want his help and I'll never be in God's Grace again. I don't care. Micah and my family have made me happier than being an angel ever did. Lucifer helped me be with the man I love. He didn't even ask me to join him. It was the old Luce, kind and thoughtful—understanding Micah hadn't meant to do what he'd done. I never shared because I've always felt like he'd one day call upon the favor he did, but he hasn't."

Phyr and I exchange glances. I'd once found a hellhound on Shawn's lawn. I had said nothing at the time because I thought Lucifer was spying on me. Could it be that he was checking up on his brother? Then it hits me. Angels kill their own offspring to coverup reproducing with a human.

"You were supposed to kill Micah and didn't go through with it," I say, already knowing the answer.

Lucinda, who'd been quiet, adds, "Is that why you were stripped of your Grace?"

Shawn glances around the room. Sometimes when people give up a little of a long-held secret, they think they've given more than they have. Spilling the whole truth takes time.

I know. I'd held my own secrets for so long.

"Micah's a nephil, unaccounted for and unclaimed, but he doesn't know it. I'd like to keep it that way."

"You have to tell him," I say. "We can keep it from the Anocracy, but he should know."

Shawn nods. "For his own safety, he should know and have his Grace. I want to be the one who tells him though."

"I don't understand. Why would the Anocracy want you to kill him?" Cian, the least familiar with angels and their b.s., asks.

The angel gives the fae a rueful smile. It must really hurt Shawn to speak ill of his brethren even now. "Nephilim who are raised outside of the guidance of Heaven come into great power with no means to control it. Some are sought by the opposition."

"Lucifer," I clarify.

Shawn nods. "Yes. He usually poisons their mind against their angelic parents and Heaven. Then he teaches them how to find their parent. Angels cannot trust their own children so—" He blows out his breath. "I saw a young nephil, guileless and beautiful. I fell in love. Instead of killing Micah, I stripped him of his Grace. Without his Grace, no angel sent could find him."

At least no angel could find Gabriel, either. Then again, neither could I, not alone.

Phyr nods when I look in his direction. He's leaning against a counter, arms folded. Unfolding his arms, he straightens. "I'll need Gabriel's hair."

SOMETIME LATER, Phyr has Gabriel's hair tied around his finger. His amber gaze sweeps over the group assembled. Shifters, the council, Jada, Rhiannon, and my cousin, Niamh, and their dragon.

"I could go alone as reconnaissance. Save your ears from any angel screeches," Phyr offers.

"Not a chance," Lance and Princess say in unison.

Princess smiles at her beta and then adds, "Our alpha will need us more than ever."

It makes sense. If Gabriel lost his Grace, his connection to the angels, and what made him a nephil, he will need a reminder that he still has his shifter family behind him.

"I'm going to open something large enough that we can all rush through, but not a permanent door. We don't know where he is."

Princess and I stand side by side, following Phyr's lead as he opens a portal. The others all gather close, an invading mob or a rescue crew depending how you look at it. My heart hammers in my chest as I fight the wave of vertigo while passing through the interstitial space of the multiverse. Magic brushes against my skin as we exit a neutral zone into hostile territory.

The thrum of music, laughter, and bodies of a milling crowd, surround us. I take a moment to get my bearings and adjust to the dim light, but I recognize where we are.

Maeve's laughter rings louder than the others. "Hello, sister. Thought you would be around, eventually."

CHAPTER
TWENTY

I spin to lock gazes with Nix and Maeve. Maeve has the same color hair and skin as me. Their features are sharper and their antlers more developed than my rack. They smile at me with a mouth that is so much like my own and our father's. I almost smile back. Almost.

Nix has hair as dark and silky as a crow's wing, and their face reflects their late mother, I assume. Tatiana's beauty had no comparison, the fae say, but Nix is an ageless kind of gorgeous. They scare me more than Maeve.

Maeve was always overt with their pranks and machinations. Nix would feign friendship or truce and then hurt me.

There was a time I longed for their love and acceptance. A small piece of me wishes it would be different. We are blood, after all. Sometimes the family you're born into is like seawater. It appears to be what you need, but will destroy you if you mistake saltwater for fresh and let it in.

The shifters and supes with me snarl at my condescending siblings, forming a circle around them and I. Maeve and Nix couldn't care less. Even with our numbers, this is Nix's faerie. They could turn us inside out and do all manner of nasty things.

I only narrow my eyes. My voice is a low growl when I ask, "Where is he?"

"He? There are many hes and shes here," Maeve drawls.

"Theys," Nix adds, "Don't forget the theys, sibling."

I take a deep breath. They'd play with my anger and mock me for an eternity. "Where are you keeping Gabriel?"

Maeve points to the ceiling.

Dread pooling in my stomach, I drag my gaze to where my sibling points.

Gabriel, naked and wings spread, is pinned to the ceiling by spikes through his hands, feet, and wings. He's alive. I know because he stares back at me.

Roxy screams in my periphery. Jada, my sweet Jada, stares; eyes and mouth open wide with horror.

Suddenly, Roxy makes no noise at all. She clasps her throat, terror in her eyes.

"I'll release your voice when I believe you've learned to stop being so loud, dreadful child," Nix says.

"Why hasn't he bled to death?" I ask dumbly, yet it's the first thing that springs from my mouth. Gabriel has a form of hemophilia. Given how long he's been gone, he should be dead.

Nix clucks their tongue. "You should know better, Tati. It's my faerie. If I don't want him dead, he won't die."

If Nix decides they want Gabriel dead, it would be a matter of snapping their fingers here. Stripped of Grace, Gabriel is no match for my siblings. Neither are those I brought a match for the gathering fae. Even Niamh and Báirseach would have trouble in a faerie they weren't born in or made. We're about to have a fight I cannot win.

Phyr sidles next to me in full fae armor. His eyes glow green with faelight. I recall what he'd said about planeswalkers not needing to follow the rules of anywhere. He's our best hope of surviving if this standoff devolves into a fight.

"What do you want in exchange for Gabriel?" I know they're going to say my life, but I want to hear it.

"You know what we want," Maeve answers.

"Name it," Phyr hisses, hand on his sword.

I nod in agreement. "I want to hear you speak your terms out loud."

Maeve laughs. "Renounce your claim on father's throne."

Nix scowls in Maeve's direction, but only briefly. My pre-fae puberty sight would have missed the look, but I have adult fae abilities now.

"I don't think I will."

Maeve opens their mouth to argue, but Nix holds up their hand, silencing our sibling. "Order Phyr to close off all nowhere doors from faerie to Earth."

I'm almost tempted to say yes. Earth doesn't need more monsters, but not all fae are monsters. There are fae who come to Earth hoping to have children, to rebuild their families. They would all have to return to faerie, few in number, immortal but without the strength or numbers they had before.

I can't say yes.

"You fear the angels' retaliation for the breaking of the truce, yet —" I force myself to look at Gabriel. He says something, but I cannot hear him over the din of the nightclub.

Not all patrons give a crap about what's happening among the high fae royals. They appear to still be having a good time. Good for them. At least, that's what I hope. I hope they're not enthralled to dance until they die—one of my siblings' favorite little pranks.

"They threw him away," Maeve says. "He's nothing but some flotsam now."

I grit my teeth. They want to provoke me.

Nix shakes their head slowly. "A shame they treat their own so poorly."

"How about this," I say. "I give you three days to gather all the fae who want nothing to do with Earth here and then Phyr closes the door to this faerie from Earth."

"Renounce your claim to the throne or close the doors to faerie."

I look around. This entire faerie is likely populated by fae escaping punishment for abandoning the war, or here for some sort of refuge. Unlike other faeries, this is a city, hard and cold as one. Fae need nature and green and growing things. This faerie is a prison. No fae would come here unless they were desperate. "Maybe I'll renounce my claim if you give me Gabriel and any fae who are here held by geas."

Maeve strikes, lightning quick. Just as fast, a blur of green light passes before me. A hot wind blasts my face and something solid hits my feet.

My sibling cries out. Their face twisted in agony as they stare in shock at a stump where their arm had been.

Phyr stands, sword at the ready to strike again.

This is it. This is when we fight each other to the death.

Nix laughs.

Laughs!

At first, it's a low chuckle, then the laugh turns into something bawdy and raucous. Dancers stop what they're doing to laugh with Nix and point at Maeve.

I grow nauseated as I realize the heavy thing on my feet is my sibling's arm. I kick it away in disgust.

Nix bends over to retrieve the arm. They laugh as they wave it at Maeve. "Maeve, Maeve, so naïve! Struck the heir and got one less pair!"

It was the worse rhyme ever. Nix waves the severed arm around, dancing away through the crowd. The fae left of their own devices. The enthralled dancers pick up Nix's tune, chanting along with my sibling.

Maeve shakes their head and then glares at our sibling's back. "Give it back!"

"What the actual fuck?" Princess says. Besides my idiotic relatives, she's the first person able to speak.

"They were always impetuous," Niamh remarks in high fae, shaking their head in disgust. "They forgot a fae could strike a member of Oberon's house if said member of the house intended to harm the crown or the heir."

I point at the ceiling, asking my cousin in high fae, "Can you get your dragon to help release him?"

Niamh shakes their head. "Báirseach will only bite the angel. Maybe char him for fun."

"Can anyone get up there?" I ask the rest in English, desperate.

"I can," Lucinda offers. Her skin ripples as she takes off her shoes and jacket. Soon, she's a winged siren, flying to the ceiling. Roxy is quick to follow, her angelic wings spreading. Jada turns into an enormous owl. One shifter from Australia changes into a bat that's the size of an elementary-school-aged child.

I glance at Phyr. "Can't you?"

He shakes his head and nods at the fae still surrounding our party. Those not under Nix's thrall watch us. As if on cue, a thin fae with white-blonde hair and mauve skin notches an arrow.

"Lower your weapon," Phyr shouts in High Fae above the revelers.

The fae ignores the warning and takes aim, arrow pointing directly at Gabriel's heart.

Before I can think better of it and change my mind, I reach with my light, grabbing the fae's mind.

Suddenly, I can see everything from their eyes, feel the bow and notched arrow in their hands. My gut is churning with nerves. *I shall be executed for this, but I want the angel spawn dead before the heir makes a deal they'll regret.*

This fae isn't against me. If I take away their will, they might turn on me. I pull out of their head.

"Fire that arrow, and I will make you feel the pain of his wounds for eternity. Not even in the Summerlands shall you find release," I say in High Fae, with all the haughtiness and grandeur I can summon. It's my best impression of my father I can manage without taking on his accent and mannerisms to the point of theatrics.

To my shock, the fae lowers their weapon and their head.

"Anyone who is here, who desires their freedom, side with me, and I will let you live in my faerie free from impunity for whatever reason that brought you here."

CHAPTER
TWENTY-ONE

Eventually Nix bores of teasing Maeve, throwing the arm at them. My other sibling reattaches their arm as if it's a doll part.

Could I do that? I can't help but wonder. Probably not. I'm not a full fae. I've seen it before, though. As a punishment, my father made a fae bite off his own foot. Enchanted, the part hadn't rotted, but the fae certainly didn't enjoy inserting their literal foot in their mouth for insulting my mother.

It takes my siblings a moment to realize the fae who had gathered in their defense are missing. All mirth vanishes from Nix's face and the cold, calculating expression I know all too well from my sibling appears. The temperature drops. The former revelers back away into shadows that seem to swallow them whole.

Malicious delight gleams in Maeve's eyes as their gaze swings between Nix and me.

A frisson skitters down my spine.

"What did you do with my vassals?"

"Your vassals?" I ask in High Fae, hoping they don't notice

Gabriel is gone, too. Arching an eyebrow, I add, "You are not High King."

"You must give up your claim. You took the vassals and the nephil," Maeve croons, wrapping an arm around Nix and pointing to the ceiling with the other, "you promised, and Danu will bind you to it."

I shrug.

"You have what you want. Why are you still here?" Nix asks.

I want the enthralled, but I know I won't get them today. It's the price for getting Gabriel and those who do not have geas on them easily. Since I can't get what I truly want, I decide to share exactly how I feel. "I'm here to tell you this: I don't want father's throne. I don't want to be High Queen. All I ever wanted is for you two to love me as much as I loved you. I don't even want that now. You've evaporated the last drop of warm feeling I've ever had for you. I'm done playing your games. The next time you come after me or mine, I will end you both. It will make father upset, but he'll get over it. I am his favorite, after all."

I expect my childhood bullies to retaliate, to play a cruel trick, or at least strike me.

Nix only looks away and whispers, "leave my faerie."

So, I do, taking the people who matter more than my own flesh and blood with me.

CHAPTER
TWENTY-TWO

I 'd thought I'd gotten away with Gabriel so easily, but there is
always a price when you break a bargain with the fae. While I
took those I'd freed from Nix's faerie to my own, Princess and
the shifters took Gabriel home. I'd meant to go to him right away but
setting everyone up with housing and duties within my faerie took
time. I trusted Gabriel would use the ways he healed before he
met me.

I was wrong.

In the pack house, Gabriel lies in his huge four-poster bed,
staring up at the ceiling. His wings are gone, put away to rest within
and heal. He's bandaged. The once-white wrappings are tinged with
blood. His skin is sallow. His features a little sharper from weight
loss. Gabriel's green eyes are dull and his gaze vacant.

He doesn't acknowledge my arrival.

Roxy sleeps in a chaise between bookcases. Her therapist will
likely have a lot of work ahead of her.

Jada has returned home, hopefully sleeping too. All my daughter's life, I'd thought I could protect her from the horrors I'd seen. I

can only hope I provide her with enough love and support to get over this experience.

"Why won't you draw from the pack to heal?"

He turns his head toward the wall. "I told you to leave me there. Now, you won't let me be in my own home."

His voice is raspy from disuse, or maybe screaming, as he was tortured by the angels and then my siblings.

"No. I won't leave you be. If you won't draw on the pack, then I'll heal you myself."

He swings his gaze to meet mine. There's anger below the sadness—no, not anger, hatred. "I don't want you to touch me. You're the reason I've lost everything. You beguiled me from the moment you first saw me, planning my ruin from the start."

"Gabriel, I don't know what you're—"

"Don't deny it!"

I flinch. Gabriel hasn't ever yelled at me before.

He holds up a bandaged hand and counts on his fingers. "First, you fed me impure thoughts about you while I was a married man. I was so fooled by your motherly act. I thought you the better mate and drove my loving wife away. What kind of person would try to fuck someone minutes after their spouse died?" His mouth twists with disgust as he mocks something I'd said out of grief and desperation, "'Take away my pain, Gabriel.' You knew how much I already cared for you. I would tear apart anyone for you. How could you not? Raf knew I was in love with you. I should have known you didn't reciprocate my feelings.

"Second, you don't love and rely on me the way you do Phyr. You let him, a supposed stranger, right into your home, make him everything in your life but your lover—or so you say. You've probably been fucking him all along, making a fool of me. Did you really lose your memory, or has this been trickery to get fae back on Earth all along?"

I take a step back, shaking my head in disbelief. None of what he accuses me of is true, but the grain of truth distorts everything else. I don't know if the angels or my siblings did this to his mind, but it's plain to me there's no convincing him otherwise.

Still, I can't let him die of wounds inflicted upon him because of me. "Let me heal you, and you'll never have to speak to me again."

Gabriel snorts. "You know what the worst part is? I could have kept my Grace if I'd given up your name. Even with the cold facts of what you are and how you used your fae powers over my mind, I couldn't do it. Not because of some geas. I'm still utterly in love with the lie. That's how I know they told the truth about your bewitchment. Leave or I'll use your name against you. Use it to own you like you own me." There's something in his expression that conveys he wants to do just that. "Go!"

I jump at his shouted command, but I don't budge. "Fine. Use my name against me. Order me to heal you. Order me to be your obedient wife. Whatever. Just don't let me let you die like this."

Gabriel closes his eyes, silent tears falling. "Please, release me from this hold you have on my heart.", he pleads weakly.

"Mrs. Diaz." Roxy's voice is hard, but her lip quivers as she rises to her feet. "My father said leave. Respect that."

I nod. He has the pack to rely on and healing him against his will would only convince him further of my evil doing.

Out in the hall, Princess gives me a hopeful look.

I shake my head because if I speak right now, I'm going to choke up.

She threads her arm through mine, taking me downstairs and out of Gabriel and Roxy's earshot.

"He thinks I seduced him to turn him against the angels." My lip is quivering now. My voice is unsteady as I continue, "He said I—"

"Shhh...Don't worry about what he said." Princess squeezes my hand as we make our way to through the massive house. It's thankfully quiet. The children are asleep, and the rest of the pack exhausted from days of searching for their alpha.

The pack beta releases a shaky breath. "He said horrible things about me, too. That I worked with you to distract him from his duties as an archangel. That I wanted him to fail and lose his Grace as revenge for my father's death. Utter bullshit. My father was an abusive prick, who told me he'd rather kill me than see me mate with a woman. Gabriel saved me from challenging him myself. I love my brother." She shakes her head mournfully. A stray tear or two stains her cheeks. The veneer of the hard-ass biker chick I met over a year ago is gone in her grief.

Princess makes so much more sense now.

Her hardness hid her soft heart.

"I don't know what it will take to get him to see to reason," I say.

Wiping her cheek with the back of her hand, Princess lends me a fragile smile. "We pray and hope."

CHAPTER
TWENTY-THREE

P hyr awaits outside the farmhouse. Gabriel's words echo in my head as the closest person to me takes my hand. My dearest friend says nothing as he cracks open time and space to take me home.

We stand in my bedroom inches apart. I don't know what he reads in my face, but I think he believes I need to be alone. He turns to leave, but I grab his wrist.

I can't speak at first. It's too painful. I have never compared the two. I love each for different reasons, and I know that they have some sort of feelings for each other, whether it is friendship or something else, we still haven't discussed. It is unfair and wrong that the angels could corrupt something good and wholesome. Hypocrisy. Angels themselves don't always partner for life—Shawn's love for Micah is an exception rather than the rule.

"Gabriel thinks I used him to get fae into this territory. He says you and I were having a secret affair all along and that I never had feelings for him. He compared how I treat you to how I treat him."

"I don't think love is quantifiable," Phyr states. "However, your love for him is different than your love for me. We have an enduring love of those in close companionship for a very long time. Our purposes will never be at odds because our purpose is the same. You burn for him, want him, and he makes you happy by existing. You have similar goals, but his purpose reaches a far broader domain than yours. You love and want to protect this community. He loves and wants to protect all supernaturals and humanity. This will cause discord, but he should know to trust you. You've proven your loyalty to him against your own siblings tonight."

As usual, my dearest friend is right. Gabriel could only be manipulated if the lies already lived in his head. "I think it's over."

Phyr places a hand on each of my shoulders. "If he was so easily manipulated into thinking the worst of someone he's known for almost seventeen years, then it's best."

Tears fall, and my friend wipes them away, as he always has.

I find myself wrapping my arms around Phyr's neck. He embraces me in return. Our mouths find each other in a soft press of the lips. I breathe in his scent, comforted by his warmth.

The kiss deepens.

My hands roam his body, and he explores mine in return. It's sweet and slow.

"We should bond now," I whisper against his skin.

"There won't be witnesses and we're on Earth."

"Will it not work?"

He shrugs. "I don't know. It's never been done this way."

"I don't want to do it in faerie. This is our home. This is where we are safe."

"Then we try here." He smiles. "I don't mind doing it twice if we must, but we'll need the land and witnesses."

"There are sprites in the garden."

He twirls me as if we're dancing, and we're in my flower bed under the moonlit night sky. Sprites, small as fireflies and glowing just as brightly as the insect, flitter among the plants. They happily tend my garden. My helpers. My tiny Low Fae court. They've seen me through so much over the years, watched over my daughter dutifully, and all they've asked for is a little cream here and there. It seems fitting they witness one more important event in my life.

Thanks to our combined efforts, my backyard is as beautiful a setting as any faerie.

I hate that this special moment is tainted by the dull ache left by Gabriel's rejection of my gift, and the worry he will not make it.

As if he is reading my thoughts, Phyr says, "He'll draw on his pack. Gabriel loves his daughter and his shifter kin too much to give up."

"Shawn," I say, glancing at the Johnson's house. "Shawn could get to him."

Phyr disappears from my arms and returns there in a blink. "Shawn has tried. Lucifer is on standby to intervene as well. He hasn't the same qualms as you do about healing him without consent."

I scowl. "How long have you been gone?"

A slow smile spreads across Phyr's lips, wicked and salacious—beautiful in its rarity until recently. "I'm an immortal planeswalker. Time is irrelevant for me, my love."

"My love," I repeat. Phyr has called me many terms of endearment, but this is the first time he's used love.

I don't know who leans in first, but I do know that it's me who unbuckles his leather armor before he slides my shirt over my head. We kiss and caress our way to fully undressing, touching places we've never dared touch before and will definitely explore later.

Naked in the moonlight, we part, taking each other in head to toe as we circle each other three times. I remember only seeing the bonding ceremony once, but a memory like that sears into your mind —unless you have a hex to haze it. Still, it's one of my recovered memories and fresh in my mind as if it had happened weeks, not years, ago.

We face each other, press palms together and swear to each other oaths as ancient as the fae themselves. I slide his long, silky hair over his shoulder to reveal the spot where the neck meets the shoulder. Vampire legends of biting there instead of the jugular must have come from humans observing fae during this ritual.

The intense need to possess him forms a hunger deep in my core —a feeling I've come to fear with Gabriel, but with my fae friend-soon-to-be-bondmate, I can relish the feeling for what it's for. Instinct meant to be pleasurable, carnal, not violent.

"Ready?" I ask in English. It's not part of the ceremony, but I want to make sure.

Phyr nods. He must now reveal his name. "Sétanta."

The name has some significance, but I don't know what. I only feel the magic of it settle into me.

"Mórrigan."

That's all I need to strike, biting into his flesh.

A sharp pain sings from the same spot on my own neck, replaced by utter bliss. His light pours into me and my faelight spills out from the cache. We're two brilliant, land-bound stars.

I don't need to tuck my power inside again after the bonding is over. My light and his, our fae souls, are one. Not even death could part us now.

Suddenly there's a cacophony of beating wings. We look above. Crows in the hundreds, perhaps thousands, blot out the moon and stars. I can feel every mind. They're the ones that usually roost at night at UW Bothell, passing over my house every evening. They're mine. All crows are mine.

Phyr swallows hard. "They mark change. The return of the Tuatha de Danann because the Mórrígan has her hound's heart. We battle together instead of against each other this time, anam cara."

His true name clicks. Many Celtic myths are fae history. Sétanta was also known as Cuchulainn or "the hound". I am the reincarnation of the goddess of war, fate, and death, and Phyr is the hound who once rejected her and died for his rejection. Neither of us remember that ancient piece of our former selves, yet we found each other.

He cups my cheek. "Now you know why I couldn't tell you my name before. Danu said you had to choose me freely."

We sink together on the garden bed, sealing the bond between us.

TWENTY-FOUR

P rincess texts me around eight in the morning. I'm in the middle of the morning rush at the bakery, so I don't see the text until I've stopped for a break around noon. I stop what I'm doing and read the wall of text she's sent twice.

Phyr sidles next to me, hovering over my phone in the office. "Any news?"

"Gabriel hasn't worsened, but he's still bleeding." I rub my forehead. "I don't understand how he's still alive."

Phyr shrugs. "Witches discovered formulas to manipulate reality and called it science, but magic is magic. I've seen nephilim with his condition survive months starved and bleeding to death."

I stare in horror, understanding he gained this knowledge in a time of war. He doesn't seem too troubled over what he shared, either.

Phyr gives my shoulder a squeeze. "What I'm saying is that he has time to stop moping and change his mind."

A bell notifies us that someone has entered the front of the shop. I put on my apron and Phyr helps me with the ties.

In the front, stands a man in his late thirties or forties with dark brown hair streaked with silver. He is dressed in the casual gear of a t-shirt and jeans, typical of the Pacific Northwest, regardless of income. The stranger's gaze takes in the shop with mild curiosity. What sets him apart from other patrons who come in for the first time is that his gaze doesn't linger on the glass dessert cases or the decorations, or the myriad of plants I have growing in the shop. He instead regards the door and walls, warded against anyone with ill-intent from entering. The wards should be visible to the naked eye, but he observes where they should be with keen interest, as if reading the spellwork.

I dip into my faelight.

The stranger is human, mostly, with thin streaks of green faelight —thinner than the green in Rhiannon's aura, and she's one-sixteenth brownie.

"Druid," Phyr says by way of greeting. "What do you ask of us?"

The one he calls druid takes a slow assessment of Phyr. The stranger's expression is one of a person much older than he appears. "I prefer no title, but mage will do. If you insist on one, please." He speaks with a slight Irish lilt. "My kin have not practiced as druid pagans since the Christians came to the Gaelic world with their iron swords and crosses."

I wonder if he doesn't want to be associated with his pagan past or doesn't like that his ancestors worshipped my kind.

The stranger directs his gaze to me. He furrows his brow. "You never called. So, I came to offer my services before it's too late."

I don't like the way this man with small magic assumes he's any help to me or supes as powerful as the Baba Yaga coven.

"Agent Tan sent you?" Phyr asks.

He spreads his hands. "More or less. I go by Gavin Doyle. Does the name mean anything to you?"

"Yes. You're the Archmage for the I.S.E.A. I reply, remembering where I heard his name before and why the title Archmage is impor-tant. So much had happened surrounding Gabriel, I'd forgotten to contact the Archmage. "I go by Miriam Diaz and my partner goes by Phyr—Brendan, in mixed company."

Archmage Doyle smiles. "Mixed company, mundane humans, I suspect. What an honor to be included in your supernatural club. Shall we get back to what is so important that you couldn't give me a call, or do you think I'm not good enough to help a halfling witch and fae?"

I don't like his tone nor the chip on his shoulder. "We've had a few things come up, Mr. Doyle."

"Two covens, at least forty witches, have perished since you met with Agent Tan. Can't imagine there'd be much more important than that."

"The archangel was dying, or would have if I hadn't rescued him," I reply. "I must also run my business to support my family." I gesture around me. "So, forgive me for not contacting you on another matter. I handle multiple at a time, you see."

Phyr snickers.

Doyle shakes his head and clucks his tongue as if admonishing a child. "Fae and their self-importance. We're all busy. However, you need me to claim this land and the other fae need my division to help protect other territories. Do you even *want* to protect this world from the warlocks?"

I close my eyes and count to three, taking deep breaths. It would be so easy to reach in and snap this druid—er—mage's mind. If I were a self-important fae, I would do that and wait for the next mage in the division to show up, take over their mind and use them as I deemed fit.

I could do it if you don't want to, Phyr says in my head.

Ha. Ha. He's just another Chad, not worth it.

It hits me as I say it. He's just like Chad, a man who served on the high school PTSA board with me. Chad had believed his time was more important, his work outside the board more important than mine. He was used to people jumping at his every command. Doyle was the government worker version of self-important middle management. I summon all the patience and diplomacy I've learned after serving for years on the PTSA with men like Gavin and Chad.

"Listen, Archmage Doyle, as a member of the Supernatural Council of the Pacific Northwest, I would like to work with the I.S.E.A., however, I don't work *for* them and never will. For any partnership to work, we will act as peers and allies, using manners and respect one would one expect from such a relationship, or we will not work together at all. Now, as I've said, I had pressing matters that kept me from contacting you. It wasn't an intentional slight. I'd also like to express my appreciation for you coming to me when I couldn't come to you."

"Well, I—" Archmage Doyle begins, a smile touching his lips. He only heard the last sentence, I'm sure.

I smile sweetly as I interrupt, "But, this is my place of business where mundanes enter at will, not a place to discuss strategy or tactics for defense against the warlocks. I'd be pleased to discuss those matters with you over dinner if you'll come to my home this evening, say around seven?"

Doyle blusters nonverbally for a few seconds. The mage has come a long way from D.C. and likely has many people under him, waiting for his orders regarding the fae. He's not used to someone else calling the shots. He also will look like an asshole if he starts making demands after I've offered my home and food. Fae and witches don't offer these things lightly, and he likely it's likely he knows this.

I keep smiling at him as if I have simply offered him to come over to dinner and I'm being perfectly sweet, and not summarily dismissed him from my place of business. "Do you have a food allergy or prefer to eat at a different time?"

Doyle blows out his breath. "No. No. Should I bring something?"

I turn up my smile. I can. I've won. "Just yourself or any mages under you that can help with the planning. I will probably have the king come as well. He'll want to hear what you have to say."

The Archmage swallows hard. "High King Oberon?"

I nod. "Yes. Father goes by that name."

The agent blinks and his mouth works soundlessly.

"I go by Miriam Diaz. My name in faerie is Tatiana," I smile, all innocence, as if I don't understand the weight of my name or that my predecessor was a formidable warrior queen and feared more than Oberon himself. "Tati for short among the courtiers."

Doyle's face pales. "S-seven works. I'll b-bring three members of my regional team."

He sketches an awkward bow and rushes out the door.

"Oh, agent Tan. You didn't tell him who I am," I sigh.

Phyr chuckles. "She must have wanted to hear about that insufferable druid making an ass of himself in front of the heir to the throne."

I smile. "I don't know her well, but I like her."

My consort returns the look. "She's growing on me as well, anam cara."

The bell rings as a customer walks in.

TWENTY-FIVE

While Phyr retrieves Oberon, Jada and I set the dining room table. It's our first moment alone since Gabriel's rescue. She pauses her duty of setting the silverware and watches me from the other end of the table, worrying her bottom lip.

I know that look. She has something on her mind, or she wants something. I will not like whichever it is, so she's brooding on how to bring it up.

"Boils left festering never heal," I say, adjusting a glass's placement—fae perfectionist to my marrow.

"Roxy thinks you never loved her dad. Says that you didn't deny any of his accusations. She says if it weren't true that you'd fight and tell him so. She says he's not getting better because no one is fighting for him."

I pause and take a deep breath to choose my words carefully. He lusted after me when we were both married and now blames me for it, but I can't tell her that nor any of the awful things he said. Nor do I want to relive those painful accusations.

"I risked my life and yours to save him. The shifters, especially

Princess, wouldn't be taking care of him if they didn't want him alive and well. If Roxy doesn't think that's fighting for him, I don't know what she wants us to do."

"You could've gone into his head and sorted out what the angels did to him," Jada suggests, but her heart isn't in it. Given our previous conversations about manipulating others' minds, it doesn't feel like something she would say. Roxy put her up to it. Sometimes Gabriel's daughter reminds me way too much of her mother Kirsten.

"I promised him I wouldn't ever use my fae gifts on him. Besides, even if I wanted to, I can't undo belief. I can only place new beliefs there. Gabriel is strong enough to fight manipulations of his mind. He has to want to fight it."

"What if he can't? What if the brainwashing is too deep?" Her voice quavers. Jada has known Gabriel for almost her entire life. He's not only Roxy's dad, but Raf's friend—a connection to the time before her father died.

I circle the table and squeeze my daughter's shoulder. "I was once very much in love with Lucifer. Believed every word he uttered. The King of Hell had me so enthralled I didn't know up from down unless he told me which was which. However, I was still me deep down. I knew in my gut that what he wanted from me wasn't right in my gut. If I can escape literal Hell with the help of one friend, Gabriel can break this hold the angels have over his mind with the support of his daughter and pack."

ALONG WITH JADA AND I, four fae: Oberon, Phyr, Niamh, and Cian sit across from four agent mages from the International Supernatural Enforcement Agency and the three sisters from the Baba Yaga coven. Together, this oddball dinner party shares grilled chicken, summer salad, and a few bottles of rosé from a Woodinville winery.

The four mages from I.S.E.A. are all men. I could have sworn being a druid didn't depend on gender. Perhaps these guys are all top brass and not an example of what the mage division looks like. That doesn't sit well with me, either. Why isn't there at least one woman present?

"My guess is that the warlocks are looking for the World Destroyer spell and when they don't find it, they kill any witch that could report to the others what's happening, then go on to the next coven," Ezma says in Kairska.

I translate, much to the chagrin of Friza and Shirom. They don't like my translation, but this is my house.

"We could set up fae and a mage to guard each area surrounding the covens between here and the last murdered coven," Agent Doyle suggests.

"Why is it important that a mage and not a witch work with a fae?" Shirom asks. "Spellwork is spellwork."

Doyle smiles at the youngest of the Baba Yaga sisters. "We are the indigenous people of this world. The soil is in our blood."

"A few thousand years and a few hundred human consorts, and our children have nothing from this place?" Ezmal asks.

This time Shirom translates, gaze briefly flicking to me. I hold up my hands.

"Excellent question, my dear," Oberon answers in English. "However, I've only seen a claiming work with those of a mage bloodline tied to the fae."

Ezmal shrugs. "Maybe we have some."

I translate for my father. Shirom and Frizma nod their approval. Gee. Thanks, witches.

"I could tell if you did," Oberon says. "Shall we investigate?"

If I didn't know better, I'd say my father was flirting with the elderly Ezmal. In fact, I do know better, he is definitely trying to ingratiate himself with the powerful witch. Granted, my father is also elderly, despite appearances.

Doyle and the other mages give each other dubious glances. Agent Doyle smiles just on the edge of condescendingly. "You might have fae bloodlines in your midst, but I doubt you have what were once druids. We keep detailed family trees."

Shirom snickers and says in Kairska, "He is so sure. Yet, if I wanted this one's seed to ripen my belly, it would be easier than milking a cow."

Friza laughs.

Ezmal waves a dismissive hand with a derisive snort.

The fae and the agents look at me expectantly for a translation. They'll wait until the end of time before I share that bit of observation.

Instead, I clear my throat. "These things are never certain. However, to save time and effort it would take to find witches with mage and fae blood, I believe we should work with the agent mages to claim the land as a form of protection."

The Baba Yaga sisters exchange glances. "We will accept for our coven, but the mages and fae will have to convince the other covens," Ezmal says and Shirom translates.

THE CONVINCING IS HARDER than I thought it would be. Through Phyr's planeswalking, I travel with Agent Doyle and his crew. Covens aren't willing to work with outsiders, and I no longer look like a witch, let alone Gracia's daughter. Perhaps that's a good thing. There is no love lost for the Archivist coven. Many ancestral grimoires found their way into the archives instead of the hands of the rightful descendants.

"We're going to have to have fae claim the land without the covens' approval," Doyle suggests.

Mage Connors, a new to me agent in her mid-thirties to early forties with sandy brown hair, a round face and full-figure, pushes up her clear-framed glasses. "May I point out that the coven's lands are warded?"

Doyle scowls and sneers derisively at Connors, then speaks to her in a tone that implies she's an idiot for making the point. "Then we break the wards."

I hold up my hand. "I'm not comfortable with that. Those wards—"

"Haven't mattered one iota in any of the attacks," Doyle snaps.

I shake my head. In order to hide my identity, the part of me that had to lie low and make very little waves for many years screams for me to leave it be, smooth things over, but I can't. He's putting people's lives in danger.

"The warlocks are our greatest concern, yes, but we can't forget the wards were put there before the resurrection of this enemy. Witches also lay wards to keep others who would do them harm off their property. "

Doyle holds up his hands. "Hey, take a breath, Miriam. I'm only trying to help here. I'm not saying leave them defenseless, just that we've got to prioritize threats."

His overt friendliness irritates me to no end. Not that I need him to call me Ms. Diaz, but he's treading on a level of camaraderie that I do not approve of. "We're not in a position to make that decision for them," I say, instead of tearing him a new one.

Doyle smiles. "You're out of your territory, but as an Archmage I have the authority to eliminate threats to the wellbeing of the public and to do so at my discretion."

"The fae will not be part of encroaching on witches' means of defense."

Doyle blows out his breath and throws up his hands, spinning around as if summoning the wisdom of the sky. "How am I supposed to help witches if you won't let me do my job?"

"We can claim all the land surrounding the covens," Connors suggests. "Also, we have a few more covens on the path to go. Maybe once one of them accepts, others will let us in."

"I agree."

Doyle swings his gaze between us and the rest of the mages.

Something must have told him he couldn't win this one because he says, "Seems reasonable."

CONNORS WAS RIGHT. After three covens agree, those who have previously chased us off change their minds and ask to work with the fae and mages. Still, there are a few covens that refuse and even place iron shavings along their borders.

There's nothing to do for them. Our strategy is to station mages and fae warriors in those places. By doing so, we're not only helping the witches, but we're taking away an advantage the warlocks gain when they kill witches and consume their light.

CHAPTER
TWENTY-SIX

We are again seated at my dinner table. This time it's a family only meal. We discuss the fae territories that will be marked out in the claiming without an outsider's opinion.

My father, High King Oberon, deems Southern California the place he will personally claim. "Close to you, my dear, but not so close that we'll impede on each other."

"I will claim the seas and rivers of the western coast," Niamh says. "You hold little sway over the waters, cousin and uncle."

"True," Oberon says with a shrug.

I nod. It makes sense. I am not a water fae and don't feel connected to water as a witch either.

My siblings and Phyr want no part in a claiming of a human territory. The latter perplexes me.

"Why don't you claim land?"

"To claim a land is a pledge to protect it. I've been a warrior and I don't care to be anymore. I shall keep our bakery running while you take your additional duties, anam cara." He raises a glass of wine.

Oberon gives Phyr a look of approval and raises his glass. "As it should be in a bond-mated pair.'"

Phyr and I toast with my father.

"So, mom is the bad ass warrior, and you're like the guy who stays home and takes care of the kids?" Jada asks.

Phyr winks. "Precisely so, kid."

With a faraway look in his green eyes, Oberon sighs. "'Tis the way of the fae. My Tatiana lead the armies against the angels while I raised Nix and Maeve, and Niamh, too, after their mother died and their father took up the sword in her place."

Who also died, I think, but don't say out loud.

Phyr, who can hear my thoughts, gives me a rueful smile. *I'll still come to your side in battle, anam cara.*

Jada passes my father a dinner roll. "That's nothing like how things work here."

"It should be," I say.

Jada grimaces. "Patriarchal religions ruining everything."

"Man using those religions to oppress others is at fault," Oberon corrects. "Gods become what their believers want them to be."

My daughter nods, her expression pensive. Her father, my former husband, Raf, is a demigod who ascended to godhood. Not all demigods ascend, but Raf had entrenched himself in this community. His light slowly built until his human form couldn't sustain it.

Fae are another kind of god, tethering themselves to a land or faerie, not becoming pure energy until their corporeal form perishes in battle or murder. Then their light moves on to the Summerlands.

"Do you think the Angelic Anocracy pushing their one-god campaign changed their creator?"

"I don't know." I truly don't. "No one has heard from that god directly in a very long time."

"It might be they gave their creator too much power. It's hard to stay in a sentient state if you're omnipotent. You'll go mad." Oberon shudders. "Keep your followers few, but devout. It's better for all."

"I wonder what mundanes talk about at the dinner table." Jada laughs and pushes to her feet.

"Lawnmowers," Phyr answers. "I dined with the Johnsons, and Micah had quite a lot to say on the subject."

I chuckle as I top everyone's wine. "Is that why you avoid their invitations?"

Phyr shakes his head. "No. I was quite fascinated with his obsession with an effort he'll never win. I stopped dining with them when the couple's eyes glazed over when I spoke of woes and triumphs of being a baker." He snorts. "They didn't know the difference between fondant and marzipan. They believed they were the same thing."

I feign disbelief but can't hide my grin. "The ingredients and process are entirely different."

"Precisely what I said." Phyr grins back over his wineglass before taking a sip.

"No difference. Sweets are for land fae," Niamh declares in heavily accented English,"and seasoning."

"Or cooked food," Oberon adds,

"A raw fish, eaten fresh from the river, is the finest cuisine one could eat," Phyr teases in High Fae.

My cousin bobs their head enthusiastically. "Yes!"

Niamh's earnest reply is too much. We all burst out laughing.

OBERON FINISHES his dinner and asks me to join him in the garden for a private chat. I agree since he is my father and a moment alone with him isn't a bad idea. I'm sure he'll have something to say about my bonding.

Fae are nothing but contradictions. Oberon cuts an imposing figure yet takes no space at all. He's a tall and willowy fae, but I know my father is strong in magic and body.

Turning to me, he says, "There is something I want to give you.

Something dear to me. In fact, my gift is the most precious object I own."

"Father—" I protest. Fae gifts are rare.

He holds up an elegant, long-fingered hand, cutting me off. A sword appears in his hand, long and covered with script in High Fae. "I had planned on giving this to Nix, but since your siblings went against my wishes and harmed the archangel, they will not be receiving any gifts from me."

"Is it?"

"Tatiana's sword. It will slay an angel in one strike. May it swing true for you."

Unlike Lucifer's offer, I cannot refuse this sword. I accept it with gratitude on my face because I can't thank my father out loud.

I am grateful. However, if the sword didn't protect the High Queen of all fae, it would do me no good. I will hide it in a cache for all eternity. There's little from the Bible I'll agree with, but I agree with the expression, "Those who live by the sword, also die by the sword."

After the guests leave and dinner is cleaned up, Phyr and I retire. We haven't changed the arrangement of sleeping in our own rooms. We haven't spoken of the bonding ceremony or what we did after the ritual. He lingers on the top of the stairs, a rueful smile on his lips making my chest ache.

"In the beginning, when I had to report to him my every move, I wished him dead and out of the way. Now, I miss our chats. Funny that."

I don't have to ask who "him" is. There is only one person who made Phyr check-in, and that is Gabriel. I take my friend's hand in mine.

"I miss him, too." I sigh loudly. "Jada thinks that I should fight, or at least try to defend myself."

Phyr wings a dark eyebrow. "You didn't?"

I swallow the lump forming in my throat. "It's not that I didn't. I felt my actions have spoken for my intentions, or at least they should."

He purses his lips and shakes his head. "You pretended to be a latent with no magic, had a spouse on the council who created those lies, and you tried to seduce Gabriel as soon as you didn't have Rafael for protection."

"Hey now!"

Phyr holds a finger to my lips. "Peace. I know you were grieving and sought solace in a handsome acquaintance's muscled arms but look at it from his perspective. He pined for you for years, had his own guilt about desiring you when he shouldn't have. Then, there you were suddenly reciprocating what he wanted, but you weren't, really. You ignore him for years, and then when you're in trouble, you initiate a relationship."

I open my mouth to protest.

"After you get his trust and affection, you ask for the fae to come into his territory. He has a lot of reasons to believe the angels and few to believe you're not what they accuse you of being."

I clamp my mouth shut.

Phyr is right, as usual.

Sighing, I say, "I'll talk to him tomorrow."

He smiles and kisses the corner of my mouth. "And tonight?"

I gently tug Phyr's hand, leading him toward my bedroom.

CHAPTER

TWENTY-SEVEN

I pull up to the shifter farmhouse, greeted immediately by wolf pups and a harried-looking Aurora. Just one little demigoddess had me looking like that. I can't imagine how hard it would be to raise four shifter pups when you're a bigfoot. Aurora, and a few other of her kind I've gotten to know over the last year, tend to be all peace, love, and happiness types with a chill vibe. The pups' biological mother is a convicted murderer, and their birth father is a former cultist, convicted of kidnapping. Definitely some mismatched energies going on there.

I embrace the tall, willowy blonde as the pups nip at the hem of my sundress. One takes the material in his mouth and shakes his head.

"Hey, what have I said about using friend's clothes as chew toys?" Aurora says in a chiding tone.

The pup drops the material and whines, pressing his muzzle and the now wet skirt to my leg.

I smile and scratch behind the wolf's ears. "Apology accepted."

Aurora squeezes my arm. "I've got to get them to the forest. They're late for a hunt with Roxy."

After I called Princess to let her know I was coming and why, she must have arranged for Gabriel's daughter to not be present.

I pat Aurora's hand. "You're doing a good job. Nice seeing you."

She smiles. "Miriam, you're a good person. If angels can truly see into hearts, he should know that."

My eyes tear up. He should.

I KNOCK on the door before I enter. Gabriel is still in bed. He has fresh bandages, but blood seeps from the wounds. The air is thick with the cloying, coppery smell of it.

"What are you doing here?" There's no bite in his tone, simply weariness.

"It's not my fault that you had inappropriate feelings for me. It's not yours either. Sometimes things like that happen. What's important is that you never acted on them, even when I tried to seduce you. That proves I have no power over you."

He stares at me but doesn't reply.

"I lied to you. I presented myself as something else until I could no longer hide what I was. I pretended I had no interest in Phyr when the truth is before I could even remember him, my heart remembered how much I loved and trusted him. I never showed you that kind of love and trust, simply because of your angelic nature. Your angelic side made me hesitate and second guess your motives. I still had the trauma of my relationship with Lucifer in my head, and you had to suffer for it. I'm sorry."

His throat works, but still, he says nothing.

"I thought of my family, my people, but didn't think of what it would cost you if you let them in. I didn't think the Anocracy would take your Grace. Part of me believed the angels would see to reason if someone like you showed them how corrupt they'd become. But, I'm not here about any of that. I'm here to beg you to get well, be a leader, and fight for your earthly family and friends."

I take a deep breath.

"I went about this entire relationship wrong and brought another person into it before it could start, but I love you, Gabriel Crowfoot. I love you and believe in you. You're stronger than whatever they took from you. Your Grace is in your desire to protect and lead. No one can take that, not even me. The only person stopping you from your full potential, from getting out of that bed, is you."

Tears run down his cheeks.

My heart leaps. I've gotten through to him!

He turns his head away. "Please don't put yourself through the pain of lies just to deceive me."

I step forward, remembering what Aurora said, "You can read my heart!"

"Not anymore," he whispers.

I stand there, wringing my hands. How would I feel if someone took my faelight or witchlight? It made no sense. I would cease to be. How could an angel be stripped of Grace and survive?

Ezmal's words echo in my head. *Spellwork is spellwork.*

Oberon never stripped me of my faelight; he couldn't. He bound it with a geas.

"I don't think your Grace is gone. I think they suppressed it."

Gabriel snorts derisively. "You weren't there. It's gone."

"I'm not wrong. I'm sure of it." With that, I leave, hopeful I can prove my theory.

TWENTY-EIGHT

S hawn answers his door in a t-shirt and Bermuda shorts. His
weekend attire the daddest thing he wears all week. He casts
a suspicious glance at Rhiannon, Roxy, Jada, and two of the
covenless witches who work for me.

"Miriam, what's up?"

I smile, hoping he'll go along with my plan. "Would you like your
Grace back?"

Shawn scratches his head. "Um, what?"

"Would. You. Like. Your. Grace. Back," Rhiannon asks, shout-
enunciating every word.

He appears even more perplexed. "Um. You can't offer that."

"Can angels return an angels Grace?"

He nods. "It has to be the will of the Anocracy."

"Not true." I gesture to Roxy. "She's a nephil, but the power of
belief that gives you Grace should be there."

"If that doesn't work, we can try a de-hexing spell," Rhiannon
offers from behind. "Worked great on Miriam."

Shawn tilts his head to the side. "You think the process doesn't
strip us of our Grace but that there's some sort of hex on it?"

I nod enthusiastically, happy he's guessing my theory. "A binding spell similar to the geas that was on my faelight."

He considers what I say and then glances over his shoulder. "You want to find out now?"

"Gabriel's life depends on it." I plead with my eyes that he'll say yes.

He glances over his shoulder. When he turns back again, he's grimacing at the sounds his children make in another part of the house. I think he's going to say no, but then he says, "Give me twenty minutes."

My smile broadens. "Okay."

He points a finger in my face. "As far as Micah knows, I have council business. I don't want to get his hopes up."

I nod at the closing door.

The witches, Roxy, Jada, and I clear the furniture from the great room into the kitchen and hall. We should probably do this spell in my faerie, but I don't know if the element of chaotic fae magic might disrupt the witchcraft.

I make a circle with Jada's old chalk on the hardwood floor. Jada and Roxy set four large candles in the cardinal directions, and smaller candles in the ordinal directions. The witches gather herbs and grind them in mortars. They sing songs in Kairska while they work. The songs and actions all have intention and light poured into them until my living space becomes sacred.

When the doorbell rings, Rhiannon rushes to fetch Shawn.

"Should I stand to the side or—" Roxy asks.

I shake my head. "You don't have witchlight, but your angelic light might help with the unbinding."

"Nice to hear *might* when your Grace is on the line," Shawn says.

"Thanks for being our magical guinea pig!" Rhiannon slaps him on the back. The muscular angel doesn't move a millimeter.

Shawn lies down in the center of the circle. The women present hold hands. We chant the words we rehearsed together.

I close my eyes and dip into my faelight, opening them again with my second sight, which allows me to see the color of magic. Shawn has a faint, angelic golden glow. It's so small compared to what Gabriel had and Roxy have, but similar to the amount of faelight I'd had left after the geas. Just enough for survival and protection, which is highly suspicious to me.

Angels have existed for eons and no one questions why they have that much Grace left after being stripped? Their absolute faith in their corrupt leaders is almost unbelievable, but so many put their trust in the wrong hands. All some need is a common goal, or a common enemy, and they'll follow a leader who promises them both better times and retribution.

We chant the words of the spell, pouring in our witchlight. Jada adds some of her gods' magic. Roxy pours in her Grace and some shifter light as well.

There's a glittery red spot in the center of Shawn's body that I've never seen before. It glows brighter as he lets out an agonized moan.

There it is, I think, *the binding spell*. I can't say so out loud because continuing the chant is important.

We chant and chant for hours. Shawn writhes in agony as the red spot becomes coils of some sort of script that looks a lot like the spellwork Lucifer taught me.

We chant until my knees are wobbly, and my throat is horse. Sweat soaks the back of my sundress and drips from my face. Everyone else is in the same state.

I can see the spellwork more clearly now, and I shift my intention to the weak spots, digging in those spaces like a thief digs a crowbar into the space where a window is cracked open just a hair. Because I'm the lead in this counter-spell, the other magic seeps into the same spots.

Shawn screams, rattling the windows, the walls, perhaps the very foundation as the binding breaks.

The spell falls away, and suddenly Shawn's angelic light is too bright.

I shield my eyes, hoping the others do, too. With the exception of Roxy and Jada, they're all seasoned witches, knowing there's magical backlash with any unhexing.

Bands of steel crush me, driving the air from my lungs.

"Thank you. Thank you. Thank you!" Shawn's whole body shakes as he sobs and embraces me.

"Well, I did a lot too. Where's my hug, big guy?" Rhiannon says.

He leaves me, laughing. The angel picks up the rock witch like she's a rag doll, spinning her in a circle.

"We can fix dad!" Roxy says, tears smearing her dark makeup down her cheeks.

Shawn nods and wraps an arm around her. "Let's go tell him."

The angel and nephil leave out the backdoor into the garden. The rest of us follow, watching their wings unfurl and the two take flight.

"Well, I'll be. We do all the work, and they just fly off without helping with cleanup." Rhiannon throws up her hands.

"Typical," another witch agrees.

THREE DAYS PASS. Gabriel doesn't believe that Shawn has his Grace back and has kicked his daughter out for "colluding with fae." Instead of moving into her mother and Dave's place, Roxy takes up Rhiannon's old room.

I make her explain what happened for the millionth time at breakfast.

"He called it a fae trick and demanded Shawn and I leave," Roxy says, stuffing a whole muffin top into her mouth. She and Jada sit at the breakfast table.

"Perhaps there's a spell on his mind and a geas of sorts on his Grace," Phyr suggests, pouring the girls some hot water for their tea.

Roxy nods. "I think so too."

"I could—" Phyr starts.

"No," I interrupt before he can finish his thought because I know what he's going to say. "No one is touching Gabriel's head without his consent. He'll never forgive us."

"She's right. Dad would want to break whatever they've done himself." Roxy turns to me. "But if he worsens, I think you should do it, anyway."

CHAPTER
TWENTY-NINE

Marymoor Park sprawls across 640 acres of the Eastside. When Jada was little, Raf and I used to take her to the outdoor movie nights and kid concerts there.

Most children pretend to be a puppy. Jada could actually shift into one. When she went through her Labrador phase, I would sometimes take her and Raf to Marymoor's giant dog park. It was as weird as it was wonderful to have my husband and child lick my hand and run off to frolic together as dogs. At least Raf didn't hump my leg, I suppose.

It's not dawn as I arrive with Rhiannon, Jada, and Phyr in tow. I park near in the lot near the dog park and walk out onto the field.

Someone is already there dressed in a long, white hooded robe with a white rope cinching the waist, an apparition in the semi-dark —the park has lighting. Archmage Doyle pushes back his hood and pulls back the sleeve of his robe, making a big show of checking his watch.

Yes, we're late, asshole.

Rhiannon elbows me. "Is hot Gandalf here for us or waiting on someone else?"

"Us," I sigh. I'd hoped he'd assign another mage to me. My thought being he'd find another, more attractive fae to do this with. The way I understood this claiming process, I'd be tied to Gavin Doyle through the land, and *that* thought did *not* appeal to me at all.

"We have very little time before the sun rises," Doyle chides.

"Shall we do it tomorrow, then?" I ask, all wide-eyed innocence in my tone and expression. I know as well as he that the warlocks have struck a coven on land not yet claimed. The death count rising doesn't look good for him.

He hands me a branch. "No. We'll do it here and now. Follow me and do as I say."

I follow him to a circle made up of branches. "Mind the rocks," he tosses over his shoulder.

In the dim light, I see cairn-like piles of rocks balanced on top of each other.

"Step into the circle. The rest of you stand back."

Doyle walks out of the light into the dark and back again, producing a chicken in a cage. He opens the cage, murmuring in a language that sounds like a cross between Irish and High Fae.

As a thin thread of dawn limns the eastern sky, he lifts the chicken in the air. The cage drops to the ground, forgotten.

The Archmage steps into the ring with me. Before I can ask what he's doing, I see the gleam of the blade as he draws it across the chicken's throat. Blood spatters me, the branches, and rocks as he sprinkles it around like a priest sprinkles holy water and chants in a haunting tongue.

The magic calls to my faelight. Calls to me.

Archmage Doyle shouts words. I repeat them, pushing my faelight into each syllable, intention focused on the land.

"I claim this land!"

I repeat the words.

At first I feel nothing, then I'm suddenly aware of every single living thing, from the beating of Doyle's heart to the hearts in the ant colony, to the birds flying nearby. I can feel the plants seeking the dawn, ready to photosynthesize the light into food. Every breath of those around are as loud as a howling wind.

Suddenly, it feels as if someone has turned up the gravity. My arms feel heavy and it's hard to hold my head up, let alone stand.

The magic of the land rips through me, thirsty and ready to slurp me down, blood, bones, and light.

It seeks Phyr through my connection. My faerie just beyond, too.

Someone is screaming.

My whole body is on fire as the land consumes me.

Something warm grips my hand, and some of the agonizing heat seeps into it. Another warm grip tightens around my other hand. Tears flow down my cheeks as I realize Jada and Rhiannon are helping me hold the land when I couldn't do it myself.

Three screams harmonize.

A cacophony of wingbeats and squawks resound above. I open my eyes to see a murder of crows circling. The myriad of corvid block the burgeoning dawn. I can feel every single heartbeat and sense every mind. To my left and right, Jada and Rhiannon hold my hands. Their eyes grow green with faelight.

I hear Doyle curse, but he's locked into this, too. He is mine. The land and all its inhabitants are mine. Their small and large magics, mine.

"Ours." Jada, Rhiannon, and I say in unison. *"The land, the creatures, the light are ours."*

Rhiannon, Jada, Doyle, Phyr, and I are at Lucinda's Cafe, the only place open at 5am, eating breakfast. I've loaded up on eggs, sausage, and sofrito covered mofongo. Jada munches on a bagel. Doyle is quite content with his coffee.

"So, we're like the mother, maiden, and crone?" Rhiannon asks, cutting into a stack of pancakes.

Doyle nods, blowing on his cup of coffee. No one even gives a man in white robes a second glance in this area. After all, he's sitting next to a woman with pink hair and antlers and a bronze man with horns. Even before supes came out, Eastsiders would think we were attending a fantasy con or Renaissance fair.

After taking a lingering draw of coffee, Doyle clarifies. "Badb, Macha, and Nemain were known as the three Morrígna Sisters, or The Morrígu."

My heart skips a beat. The names are a variation of mine.

Doyle continues without noticing my expression. "Other legends say the Mór-Ríoghain was a three-aspect goddess of fate and war, associated with the ban sidhe."

"I'm one-sixteen brownie, not a banshee!" Rhiannon protests, waving her syrup-laden fork in the air. "I'm clean and like house-keeping."

Jada snorts.

I bite my lip, so I don't laugh.

To avoid a nasty fae eating her, Rhiannon was covered in filth when we met her. She also was terrible at housekeeping.

"You must be a little more than one-sixteenth fae to have helped claim the land like that. After hearing that scream, all of you have ban sidhe blood, I bet," Doyle says, tipping his coffee mug precariously in Rhiannon's direction.

Rhi twirls her knife in her hand with a wicked gleam in her eye, "I bet."

Jada stirs honey into her tea. "Well, I'm the maiden and mom's obviously the mother. Which sisters will that make us?"

"Hey! I'm no crone,' Rhiannon gripes. "I don't have a wrinkle on me!"

"You *are* the eldest," I jibe and stick out my tongue.

Doyle smiles. "The three aspects aren't necessarily about age, but all three of you are now tied to the land. You'll have to stay in close contact to have the land on your side as you fight the warlocks."

"Guess I'm moving back in for a bit," Rhiannon says cheerfully. "I was kind of getting sick of rooming with two dudes, anyway."

CHAPTER

THIRTY

The bed shudders, waking me, right before something hits my bedroom window. The glass shatters, spraying the floor. I spring out of bed on the opposite side and gather my faelight from my internal cache, ready to shield against attack.

"Who goes there?" Great. I sound like a freaking castle goblin in my father's faerie.

Instead of invading warlocks, my siblings, or an angel assassin, a black cauldron the size of my refrigerator hovers outside my window. Shirom sits inside with a ladle, steering the thing.

I pack my faelight away. "What the f—"

Phyr bursts into my room in full armor. He's followed closely behind by Rhiannon and Jada, still in their pajamas.

"They're here!" Shirom cries, interrupting me.

"What's happening?" Roxy asks sleepily from somewhere in the hall, out of sight.

"Warlocks," I say. "Call the others."

With Phyr's planeswalking time-defying help, shifters, the members of the Supernatural Council of the Pacific Northwest, covenless witches, low fae, and cryptids all gather in the forest near Snoqualmie Pass.

"They've come, not for the witches," I say to the crowd, "but for our home. No matter if we have teeth, fangs, or wings, the warlocks are our enemy."

We descend upon the Baba Yaga coven's clearing. Smoke fills my nostrils as I take in the sea of white witchlight with streaks of magenta. Some of the beautifully painted Russian boyar-era-esque cottages are reduced to ash. Some are still aflame. Witches in cauldrons and warlocks straddling broomsticks zip through the air. On the ground, witches in robes and warlocks dressed in tunics out of the middle ages cast spells and counter spells, attacking like a cosplay of Dungeons & Dragons.

Except, people are actually dying.

War.

The word settles in my bones. An ancient sadness accompanies a fierce need to protect these people.

Mine.

"Group one!" I shout, sick to my core at sending anyone into the fray, but this is *our* home.

With Princess at the lead, the shifters charge into the chaos, fangs bared. Thanks to charms the Baba Yaga coven made for them, they have some immunity to spells the warlocks cast. They work with the witches as we've planned.

"Group two!" I shout in High Fae.

Niamh shouts a battle cry in High Fae. The fae who live in this territory follow. Their armor, swords, axes, and bows and arrows glimmer with green faelight. Báirseach takes flight, burning warlocks one by one with a torrent of dragon flame.

I pray to Danu that the dragon doesn't burn anyone on our side.

My chest clenches as Phyr charges, flaming sword swinging.

I stand with Jada on my left and Rhiannon on my right, waiting for our cue from the Baba Yaga coven.

"Feels weird being a secret weapon," Rhiannon whispers.

Ezmal swoops in on a cauldron. Her hair is disheveled, and her face is green with some powdery residue. The resemblance to a cartoon witch would be hilarious if blood didn't trickle from her temple. The elderly Ezmal, with powerful witchlight, has genuine fear in her eyes.

"Challenge their leader and they'll all crumble. He's called Braha. Show no mercy or this plan will fail."

She flies off before I have a chance to respond.

A warlock breaks free of the melee, hurling a blast of magic at us. On instinct, I murmur a counter defense that shatters and dissipates, useless against his stronger witchlight. I take the hit, staggering backwards without falling.

The warlock's eyes widen when I don't go down and then he takes in my horns. He says the word for demon in Kairska.

I remember what I am, drawing my faelight and letting it glow through my eyes. "No darling, I'm much worse."

The warlocks have never seen a fae. Never battled one. They likely think that they're the scariest thing around. I'm going to show the warlocks why the angels feared us so much they tried to annihilate us. As easily as I open my front door, I enter his mind. It would be oh so easy to snap it and turn him into a drooling moron. Instead, I poison him against his warlock brethren.

I seek more minds, turning warlock against warlock while searching for Braha.

A fiery green blade splits a warlock in two in front of me. Phyr grimaces at his gruesome work from behind.

"Gross!" Rhiannon says, on the ground next to me. She must have gotten hit by a blast of witchflame. Her shirt is torn, and I can see her charred flesh.

I offer her a hand to help her up and pour healing light into her. "You, good?"

She nods.

"Where's Jada?"

The rock witch points at my daughter, who is in panther form, mauling a warlock.

I shake my head, dread pooling in my stomach. This isn't how this is supposed to go. We're supposed to stay here together. I can only hope everyone remembers the most important cues.

"Use Tatiana's blade!" Phyr shouts as he dives back into the fight raging before us. He's like twirling dervish, slicing through warlocks as if it's a dance.

Right. I have a weapon. A weapon that will cause a distraction until we set our trap.

"Stay close." I say to Rhiannon.

Jada, done with the warlock, returns to my side.

"Swipe at them like P.C. bats his toys, but stay close."

My daughter cocks her panther head—as if to make sure she heard me right. Yes. I gave her battle instructions with a house cat as an example of how to fight. No. It's not a bad plan.

I draw Tatiana's sword, raising it to the sky like She-Ra. It's so bad ass. Too bad I don't really know how to use it.

"Braha, I challenge you," I shout in Kairska, amplifying my voice with the light I channel from the land.

"Oh, that's a neat trick!" Rhiannon also channels light from the land to amplify her voice.

No. No. I need her lucid, not *playing* with powerful magic.

Before I can give Rhi a piece of my mind for using the land so recklessly, a massive warlock emerges from the sea of fighters. He's almost as big as the Fremont troll, all sinew and muscle under a tunic with gold and blue embroidery around the neck and hem. A diadem circles his head. A king? Not only is the newcomer physically massive, but the warlock also brilliant white with witchlight, magenta limning his aura.

He's a borderline god, very close to ascension.

"Shit. You're a giant," Rhiannon says, breaking the silence.

Jada shifts back to human form. A sneer on her lips, she *manifests* clothing. I've never seen my daughter display this gift.

While the warlock ogles my daughter—gross—I attempt to enter his mind and find out quickly the diadem isn't just a marker of distinction. It's spelled with protection magic my gift can't circumvent.

"You. You're the one," he says in Kairska, pointing at me. "A demonic monstrosity who took my spell."

"That spell was never yours," I reply, trying to break past the spellwork of the diadem. This guy is bad news. The warlocks' belief in him has made him and his spellwork way overpowered.

He snickers, as if he can sense my attempts to get in and break his mind. I don't need to be in his head to know he finds my attempt as amusing as a child trying to drive a car, not understanding they need to reach the pedals.

"Give me back the World Destroyer, and I'll let the three of you live as my concubines."

"Oh wow. He's a real charmer," Rhiannon murmurs.

That's the world the witches destroyed. A world where they served the warlocks as their wives and concubines, nothing more than chattel. They had to practice magic in secret. They came up with the World Destroyer to free themselves, and this asshole wants to use it for his own purpose.

I see Phyr moving toward the warlock in my periphery. I think at him, *Leave this to me.*

"I destroyed the spell," I say out loud in Kairska. "It will never do harm again. Now leave this world or I will spare none of you."

Braha chuckles, his whole body shaking with the movement, as if my threat is the funniest thing he's ever heard. No wonder witches killed these assholes off—mostly. They seem to have missed a few.

"No. This world must end so that I may become powerful enough to rebuild mine." To the other warlocks, he says, "Kill the ones who can't bear children. Take the rest prisoner."

The battle picks back up again in full force.

I take Rhiannon and Jada's hand.

"Retreat!" Phyr shouts in High Fae, and then English.

Shifters and witches all run to a designated point, disappearing into thin air. Fae and the more powerful witches stay at the edge, fighting the warlocks to bar them from entering the nowhere door. Phyr built one as an escape plan for the Baba Yaga coven weeks ago, soon after the funeral for my mother's coven.

Finally, the fae and witches also retreat. As planned, warlocks follow. Too bad they don't know they're running right into my faerie, where they'll have no power.

Braha watches, eyes narrowed. However, he doesn't seem concerned that his men are disappearing. Perhaps he believes it's some sort of illusion, or that they planeswalk through spells, so he believes they'll soon return.

I don't care what he believes. I have him alone. It's time to get this battle of the Pacific Northwest supernaturals versus alien warlocks over and done with for good.

"*One last chance to retreat,*" Jada, Rhiannon, and I say in Kairska, drawing from the land. The voice coming from our mouths is not the three of ours combined.

It's the last thought I have as Miriam.

I am the rage behind the tears of every woman who has ever suffered at the hands of an abuser. I am the woman who was cast aside for another by a fickle-hearted lover. I am the grieving mother who didn't have enough food for her children because the lord took too much for his tithe. I am the woman who never saw her wedding day because her lover died fighting for a rich man's ambitions. I am the lonely woman whose children forgot her in her old age. I am the screams of the women burnt at the stake for their beliefs.

I am the Mórrígan.

"You are nothing," the warlock spits. "Women with some cute tricks. Nothing at all. It is you who will surrender to *me.*"

And of course, even as a goddess incarnate, I still have a man telling me what to do.

"*Maybe alone, this is true, but we are the sisters three: mother, maiden, and crone. We have claimed this land in the ancient way of our kind. Do not cross us. Leave and you shall be spared."*

Braha laughs. "Witches always find importance in their position in relation to us. You cannot be a maiden or a mother without a warlock to make you one."

His laughter dies on his tongue as the three of us draw from the land and scream. The ban sidhe wail renders the meat and viscera from the bones. The skeleton stands for a second, teetering before crumbling to ash.

The white and magenta light of what was once a powerful being seeps into the ground, replenishing what we took.

I'm once again me, holding hands with Rhiannon and Jada.

"That was—" Rhiannon begins.

"Disgusting," Jada finishes.

"Abhorrent," I agree, feeling nauseated by the sight.

"Psssht! Whatever." Rhiannon rolls her eyes and waves her arms dramatically. "That was so cool!"

THIRTY-ONE

I release Jada and Rhiannon's hands, taking a moment to orient myself. I look at my daughter, expecting to see horror on her face. Instead, I see resolve.

"I know you say there's no such thing as good and evil, but he was evil, mami." Jada shudders.

"Worse than the devil," Rhiannon agrees, shaking her head at the remains.

"A devil is only a devil by their actions. We still have to deal with the lot of his followers."

Relief illuminates Phyr's face as the three of us enter the faerie.

Warlocks sit in cages made of gnarled tree branches, very similar to what Rhiannon had kept the cryptids in. Funny that. Phyr must have made the originals and gave Rhiannon power over them. He also has control of my faerie through our bond, which means I have some over his, as Tatiana and Oberon had control over their respective faeries.

"I know you said to keep as many alive as possible, but it simply wasn't possible for a few." He gives me a look that says he's not sorry about killing any of them.

I arch an eyebrow. "What did you do?"

Phyr lifts his hands in surrender, his expression all innocence. "I did nothing. They, however, believed they could burn a faerie tree with their witchflame. I had to take their ability away before they burned themselves to a crisp."

I shake my head. "So powerful. So dumb."

Phyr laughs. "They think I'm a demon."

"No exposure to the fae," I reply. That was our advantage over Braha, over them all. If the warlocks had any sense, they would have researched the supes of Earth before launching an attack.

Other worlds might mind their business, but not my territory.

Rhiannon joins in.. "Seems like you'd research a world before you tried to burn it down, but that's just me."

Princess approaches in human form. She's naked. I try to keep my eyes on her face. I'd have to be dead to not notice how beautiful she is head to toe.

She shakes her head. "I don't have to speak Kairska to know they're all perverts. A thousand years in faerie might cool their heads."

Ezmal, Shirom, and Friza break from a group of witches seeing to the injured's care. Ezmal gives me a questioning look.

"Braha is crow food," Rhiannon says.

The coven leader's eyes narrow on the rock witch. She places her hands on either side of Rhiannon's head and kisses each cheek, murmuring blessing. "I hope my son makes you happy and gives you many children to care for you in your old age."

Rhiannon stammers for a minute. "Thanks?"

"Would you consider living among us?" Frizal asks as she and Shirom gather around the rock witch.

"I—I'm so sick of living with two dudes. They're great, but ugh. It's been so nice crashing at Miriam's place. I need some femmes around," she confesses. "If Lance and Daystar agree to come too, sure."

"Let us find my son and his friend," Ezmal says with a wink. "We will see to their agreement together."

As they leave, the Supernatural Council of the Pacific Northwest gathers around me.

I gesture to the prisoners,. "I don't want to be responsible for their care."

"We should turn them into I.S.E.A.," Lucinda suggests. She's back in human form and wearing a t-shirt and shorts.

"No. I don't want them on Earth," Shawn disagrees. "They are a threat to the welfare of anyone who comes in contact with them."

Princess sides with him. "Those warlocks are powerful as fuck outside this faerie."

"Let's vote on it," Leilani says.

Cian and Aurora nod in agreement.

"All in favor of turning them into I.S.E.A. to handle," Lucinda asks, raising her hand.

I raise my hand. So does Leilani, Cian, and Aurora.

"Five to two."

Shawn blows out his breath. "Okay, but they stay here until we have some way of containing their magic."

I flag some pixies flying nearby. "Find me a dryad."

Soon a tree with a not-quite humanoid body scuffles to me.

"Make sure the prisoners are fed, walked, and watered until I return. You shall be rewarded if they are all alive when I arrive," I command. It doesn't feel right to not use Earth manners, but I cannot ask. I am queen. They are fae. An ask would indebt me.

The dryad nods and slants a bow.

CHAPTER
THIRTY-TWO

Agents Tan, Roanhorse, Archmage Doyle and his mage lackeys all gape. Their gazes swing about, not stopping on one flower, strange tree, sky, nor pixie, brownie, hob, gnome, or dryad for very long.

Agent Tan speaks first. She gestures to our surroundings. "You made all of this?"

I smile. "Mostly. I seeded what this is, and I can change reality here at my whim."

Her partner, Roanhorse, looks like he's about to be ill.

Archmage Doyle kneels and touches a flower. "My gran would roll over in her grave if she knew I let a sidhe take me to a faerie."

He says it in modern Irish, but I can understand every word. So can his fellow mages, because they all murmur some sort of agreement.

"Only because the memory of what druids and the Tuatha de Danann were to each other was tainted with the stain of the empires that overthrew your people," Phyr says. In the next breath he adds, "The prisoners are ready."

"They will be powerful once they cross the threshold into Earth," I warn.

"Couldn't you just make a prison for supe criminals in the interstitial space?" a lesser mage asks. "You're fae."

I shake my head. "I don't want to waste my light on the imprisonment of criminals. These warlocks and other supes may do better with some rehabilitation."

"We'll bind them temporarily, as planned. No need for faeries. Our prison will hold anything," Doyle says with a warning look at the rest of his mages.

"It'd be easier if you'd just allow me to create a door to this prison," Phyr suggests.

"No supernaturals outside the I.S.E.A. are allowed within," Agent Roanhorse says in a tone that broaches no argument, folding his arms across his wide chest.

Phyr releases the warlocks in batches. Some resist the binding, but all they can do is squirm and physically fight. Agents Roanhorse and Tan are pretty damn good at restraining the warlocks without our assistance.

They line them up, and we take them back to Earth, loading the warlocks in unmarked vans.

Agent Tan takes me aside for a private conversation. "There's something I need to know. Femme to femme, why would you bother with this world and all its patriarchal nonsense when you could live in a faerie of your own making and your own rules for the rest of your life?"

It's a good question. One I don't take lightly. I choose my words and reason carefully.

"I grew up in a faerie and have been around the multiverse, visiting many, many worlds. However, Seattle's Eastside is my home. I raised my daughter here. My friends live here. This community is mine for better or worse, and I intend to protect it."

CHAPTER

THIRTY-THREE

Turning in the warlocks isn't the only work left after the battle. Once again, I find myself at a mass funeral. Ten supernaturals died in the fight, and many more witches from the Baba Yaga coven. We build a pyre for them near the erstwhile battlefield. My crows had left those affiliated with me, but the warlocks who died had nothing left but skeletal remains. Witches collect those bones. I do *not* ask what they'll do with them.

Two shifters died in the battle, including Nate. I hadn't particularly liked Nate but didn't want him to die. Also, Lord Feidhil, who had visited my shop. He had survived the angelic wars and recently immigrated hoping to start a family on the Eastside, but lost his life in the fight to protect his new community, to protect me. He'd addressed me as Princess Tatiana the one and only time I met him.

I say a special prayer to Danu. Phyr and I perform a rite that will send the fae off to the Summerlands.

Fae, shifters, witches, and members of the council all take a lit torch to the pyre, saying their own prayers and their own goodbyes. Then we mourn the way of many peoples. Around the pyre, we share stories, sing songs, and feast as one community united.

At some point in the evening, I notice my siblings stand at the edge of the gathering, observing. I walk out to Maeve and Nix, readying myself for another fight. Phyr joins my side. Jada finds her way from the wake to me as well. I bet if I turn around, Rhiannon would be right there. In my periphery, members of the council peel themselves away from the funeral feast. Ezmal and her sisters aren't far behind.

I lift my chin, staring down my nose at my siblings. "Why are you here?"

"We want to bid farewell to our friend, who has embarked upon the journey to the Summerlands." Maeve's eyes are wet and there's genuine grief in their features.

Nix adds somberly, "We also wanted to tell you we are closing the nowhere door in Fremont."

Maeve sneers, grief forgotten. "Do not open a new one or we shall have war, sibling."

Briefly, I wonder how Jørgen the bridge troll feels about this change and what it will mean for him.

Next to me, Phyr stiffens. Fand, his former lover, is a planeswalker and indebted to my siblings for abandoning the fae during the war with the angels. They would be the one to close the door. One of my siblings has Fand by a geas on their soul. Fand is one of many who inhabit Nix's faerie. The thought ignites a fire in my belly.

"I don't care what you want or what you do. You tortured my—" I pause, searching for the right word to describe Gabriel, now that we're no longer together. "—friend and keep fae as prisoners in your faerie. You're not welcome here."

"Everyone who comes to my faerie does so of their own volition. What happens in my faerie is done with prior consent," Nix says. "Even your *friend* asked for us to take him. You should be grateful. He wanted to die. We only tortured him a bit."

I flash them a fang-filled grin. "I'll show my gratitude by allowing you to leave with your heads."

163

Clouds roll over the night sky, darkening the night in the places not lit by the funeral pyre. Cold rushes in on a breeze that chills my blood. Every instinct tells me that trouble, not a storm, is brewing.

I'm not the only one to notice.

My siblings exchange glances, disappearing into the shadows of the night.

Cowards.

Eight shooting stars hurtle to the ground. Except they're not shooting stars, they're fiery swords in the hands of angels. Instead of white, flowing robes, the angels wear form fitting bodysuits, a few in the primary colors and the rest in brighter tertiary shades.

Rhiannon snorts. "Who called for the fancy Power Rangers?"

"Seraphim assassins," I say, wishing for anything but this to be happening right now.

Phyr swears under his breath. Angel's Bane illuminating a brilliant emerald with his faelight. My cousin Niamh cries orders somewhere behind me. Báirseach takes flight, screeching. The rest of the fae retrieve blades, axes, and crazy looking bows and arrows from caches, firing them up with faelight.

The angels don't hesitate in their attack. There's no negotiation or posturing. They simply bulldoze their flaming way from the four cardinal directions and crosswinds—a take-no-prisoners slaughter.

Save for Gabriel, everyone I love is here. I will not let that happen.

The witches, the greatest in number here, face the southern seraphs.

They would smite us all, but this ground is heavily warded and claimed. On this land, we are the predominant force. I revel in the shock in the angel's eyes—only for a moment.

My cousin Niamh charges the eastern side angel, their dragon swooping down, roaring green and gold flame.

Lucinda, in siren form, flies due north. Shawn flies after her, a flaming sword and renewed Grace at his call. A bigfoot, lizard Leilani, and a giant honey badger follows. The entire council joins in the fight, except for me.

I have my own problems.

The northwestern seraph spins like a Tasmanian Devil toward me, making just as much noise as the cartoon.

Jada grips my hand. "Mami, should we?"

I nod, shouting over my shoulder, "Everyone except Rhiannon! Stand back."

Rhi grips my other hand. The land grips us, fortifying the three into one.

Our scream cuts through the angel's defenses, enough to land a blow, slashing through their magenta tunic like a blade. The seraph produces a shield of golden glowing letters, spellwork manifested into a substance that blocks the sound.

"Well, shit," Rhiannon gripes in her own voice.

Shit is right. The angels have counter spells for ban sidhe wails.

Phyr slices through the counter magic with Angel's Bane. His face is a mask of fury. He shouts, "Shield us!"

I take Rhiannon's and Jada's hands in mine. "This is our home."

At first it comes out of my mouth. Then the words come out of all our mouths as the Mórrígan.

"This is our home!"

The golden word shield flickers. Markings fizzle out like a dead lightbulb.

"We will protect our home, our people, our right to live and worship as we please."

Every word uttered as the Mórrígan, drawing from the power of the land, tears at the spell.

The seraph advances, blazing sword swirling, the other hand reaching out with the battered spellwork shield.

"We will protect our home, our people, our right to live and worship as we please."

The angel's shield breaks off bit by bit as we repeat our stance. Around us, chaos ensues as every mourner fights. Though we are focused on our own battle, we as the Mórrígan can also aid our friends, protecting them with the light from the land.

The seraph strikes. Before the sword imbued with gods' magic can slice me in two. We three burst from our bodies into a myriad of crows. Suddenly I can see from many angles and witness all the fights.

Phyr has joined the fae, except he doesn't resemble the friend I know and love. Through our connection and the connection to the land, he has become the Mórrígan's hound, Cuchulainn, and he's fighting like him. His features are twisted and hideous, one eye bigger than the other. He's grown at least a foot taller. A berserker, slicing and stabbing too fast for the angelic assassin.

The supes use their separate strengths to fight the seraphim. The Baba Yaga witches fly in their cauldrons and cast attack spells and counterattacks to the angels.

My body of crows screech and caw as we see a witch fall to a blue seraph's sword. We descend, swarming the angel. Crows peck at the blue angel's eyes and face. More crows attack Blue's hands and tender bits behind the legs.

From the crows in the air, I see the witches back away, giving us a wide birth...and an opportunity. A tendril of our white witchlight digs into the ground from one of the crow's talons. The earth trembles, cracking open like a maw, swallowing the seraph. The crows narrowly escape before the maw closes.

From a high vantage point of my body of crows, I see Aurora in her bigfoot form, wrestling an angel to the ground.

Roxy and four shifters, all in animal form, surround another seraph. The white wolf is the seraph's focus.

The angel dodges an attack from a honey badger and goes in for the kill.

The crows descend, but we may be too late.

Just then another white wolf, twice as large as Roxy, attacks the seraph from behind, felling the angel like a tree onto their own sword. Roxy dodges out of the way. The white wolf howls. Magic pulses against my feathers. The wolf is part of this land, so I feel him through my connection to it and know it is Gabriel. He's chosen a side. He's facing the angels as a wolf, as one of his mother's people, part of this land long before I bound myself to it.

Wolf eyes burning bright with alpha magic meet the crow's eyes.

I've chosen this land, but it's part of his blood and bone, no matter how far from it he was born. This is why he wanted change, not for power or glory. This is why losing his Grace hurt him so, not because he wanted to be an angel. He is a guardian of this world and its people in the truest sense. He wants to be strong to protect his people.

I hope he sees now that his trust in the part of me who is Miriam is put in the right place. The hope turns into reality. I feel his trust and love as surely as I can feel Phyr's wrath as he fights angels.

I also feel deep sadness. Like Lucifer, he doesn't want his angelic brethren to die. He wants peace and for them to give up some of the power.

The crows coalesce into the shape of a giant woman.

"Leave!" the Mórrígan shrieks.

I push my faelight into the ground, finding the green and growing things. Blackberries are common in the Pacific Northwest. Rubus ursinus is indigenous, but Armeniacus and Rubus laciniatus are invasive. The thick, thorny vines sprout and spread like wildfire. Blackberries can survive both flood and drought. I find a single root and push my faelight into it, giving back to the land.

Monstrous vines spring up, ensnaring the seraphim assassins. They can't fight against these blackberries. This world, this land, isn't theirs to conquer and control. The earth itself is rejecting them.

Cuchulainn morphs back into Phyr, who makes quick work of dispersing the trapped angels to only he knows where.

My work done; I collapse the moment I become Miriam again.

CHAPTER
THIRTY-FOUR

Huddled together in a group and still wrapped in blackberry vines, the seraphim assassins, including the one covered with dirt Phyr must have recovered from the ground, glare at us. That's all they can do. Angels are as helpless as a newborn babe in my faerie.

I am myself, flanked by Phyr and Gabriel. To Gabriel's right are Princess, Roxy, Shawn, and the rest of the council, saving Lucinda. She stands to the left of Phyr, along with Jada, Niamh, two of the covenless witches, and the three Baba Yaga sisters.

Gabriel steps forward. His hand morphs into a clawed nightmare, slashing blackberry vines covering the mouth of a seraph assassin. The shifter alpha is not careful. The angel's sculpted cheek bleeds from a deep gash.

The skin doesn't heal right away, but I allow that small magic. I'm not here to hurt them, even though they wanted to kill me and mine.

"This is what I want you to tell my father," Gabriel begins. "We, the Supernatural Council of the Pacific Northwest, will no longer tolerate an angelic presence in our territory."

Princess holds up her finger. "We will allow the mundanes their churches as long as those churches don't infringe upon the rights of the residents of our territory. "

Lucinda's voice rings loud and clear as she all but sings, "If a church oversteps its authority, we will ask the leader of the church to leave our territory with the help of the mundane organization I.S.E.A."

"If the angels come again, we will not be so lenient," Leilani warns.

"We will call upon our allies, and you will see a war like no other," I say. "Because we will not stop until you rue the day you ever stepped foot on our planet."

"We will call upon the land, the air, and the sea, for it is our world," Aurora says, human glamour back in place. "Our mother."

WHILE PHYR TAKES the angels back, Gabriel asks everyone if we can have a moment alone. I'm exhausted from becoming the Mórrígan, but I agree. We're long overdue for this conversation. We find a clearing away from the others. The night sky in the mountains is beautiful and the air is fresh despite the pyres still burning.

Gabriel rests a palm on a tree, his head is bent. "There's been so much loss lately."

I nod, unsure if he can see me.

"The Seraph Order got in my head, Miriam. Rooting around for your name, for anything to weaken me. They found what they thought was my weakness, but you're my strength. None of what I said while I was still under their influence was true. I wasn't myself. I don't think that way. I don't feel that way. For fuck's sake. The brainwashing was ridiculous. Kirsten cheated on me. I didn't leave her for you."

The tree creaks under the pressure of his hand pushing against it.

"How did you break free of their spell?"

He meets my gaze. Tears glisten on his cheeks in the moonlight. "Lucifer. Shawn couldn't see the lift they put on me, but he could."

I cover my mouth.

"Lucifer said he didn't do it for me. He did it as a gift to you and that I owed it to him to tell you."

I bark a laugh. "Of course, he did."

Gabriel shakes his head. A small smile breaks through that melts my heart. "He saw what you did for Shawn and wants you to do it for him."

"Of course, he does." I blow out my breath. "Do you?"

He flexes his fingers. "Oh, fuck yeah. I also have a plan to stop them from ever doing it to another nephilim again."

I move closer, step by tentative step. "Oh yeah?'

His hands find my hips. "Do you forgive me for the things I said under enchantment?"

How could I not? I knew what it was like to not know the truth, to act under the influence of a hex and geas. I'd lived years that way.

I tilt my head back to offer him my lips, whispering, "Of course, I do."

His mouth crushes mine in a bruising kiss. His hands grip my hips hard, as if afraid of letting me out of his grasp.

I'll fill him on everything that transpired later. We have a different kind of catching up to do now.

THIRTY-FIVE

I straighten a teacup on the table. Pixies mimic me, turning all the teacups on the table so the handles are all at the same exact angle.

Rhiannon makes a clucking sound. "Are you and the light sprites going to do that with all three hundred of them?"

I shoot the rock witch a scowl. She knows how important this event is to me.

"Incoming!"

Jada brings a steaming platter from the kitchen, where Phyr is hard at work putting finishing touches on the formal dinner. I've used spellwork and fae magic to enlarge my dining room into a ballroom. We'll need it. We have important guests coming.

Candelabrum float and twirl in the air, dancing to unseen fae musicians. Shifters and fae usher things two and fro.

The council arrives a few at a time. First Gabriel, Princess, and Aurora. Roxy is also with him. She and Jada will present for this meeting as witnesses and the council's next generation standbys. I direct her to the kitchen, where she'll be helping fae of all manner.

Shawn arrives next. He has Micah with him as his auxiliary.

Micah kisses me on the cheek. "We have a lot to catch up on."

My friend then gives me a look that says he knows a lot more than he used to. I miss his innocence, but his innocence protects no one. We cannot hide from problems and expect them to go away; I learned that the hard way. He adds in a lower voice, "Including our entire lives before we met and some in between we've left out."

I grin at my handsome neighbor. "I look forward to it."

Lucinda comes next. She's in the full regalia of one of Persephone's soldiers. She stands with me and Rhiannon to greet the others.

Cian and Leilani enter with a stack of envelopes. The couple is radiant with happiness. The demigoddess announces what I already figured, "Wedding invites finally arrived!"

Cian grins from ear to ear. "My love couldn't wait to mail them."

I doubt Cian could wait either.

I take mine graciously, sneaking a tentative glance in Gabriel's direction. I know this is the life he wanted. A wife, children, but we have a unique arrangement.

His gaze shifts to meet mine and then he smiles, mouthing, "I love you."

He does. He's proved it. He's apologized for the things he said when he'd lost his Grace. He knows his crush on me was all him.

Maybe it's a little me subconsciously reciprocating all this time, too, but I leave that alone. Past me isn't my problem. What I do today is.

Phyr comes in with a ladle, offering something for Gabriel to taste. I won't put up with his fretting, but Gabriel doesn't mind.

Even after learning that Phyr and I bonded in every way, Gabriel is still in love with me; Miriam the mom, Tati the heir, and even the scary part of me that is an aspect of the goddess Mórrígan. Although we don't have a man, woman, child relationship like Raf and I had, Gabriel, Phyr and I are closer than Raf and I ever were. Raf and I wanted different things, and that's okay. Sometimes relationships don't work out, but they're worth the time spent and lessons learned.

Phyr, Gabriel, and I do want the same things: our two kids, Jada and Roxy, to be happy, our community to be safe, and the relationship to hold no secrets.

Gabriel approves the dish, gently squeezing Phyr's shoulder. A look passes between them that sets butterflies off in my stomach. How our intimate dynamics look beyond that, is between the three of us and not for anyone else to judge.

The Baba Yaga coven sisters and Daystar are the first non-council members to arrive. Next, the Olympian delegates Apollo and Artemis arrive. The twin's human forms are the epitome of athletic grace.

I try to hold back my grimace. It would be better if Zeus and Hera showed up. To my surprise, the queen Hera arrives with Triton. I make no comment, but Lucinda, who comes after, whispers, "Uh oh. Looks like Hera and Zeus are on the outs again. I better tell my queen to prepare for trouble."

My father and a few of his court arrive. My siblings are banned from this territory, but they wouldn't show their faces here, anyway.

More deities from other pantheons show.

Aidoneus and Persephone arrive. The king of Hades is twice as large as his human-sized queen. They eye decor, murmuring something in what is likely ancient Greek.

Lucinda excuses herself to speak with her queen.

Coyote, in the guise of a man, arrives. Well, mostly a man. If I regard him just so, I can make out fur and a tail. Arriving with him is a crow person who doesn't hide their true nature. They regard all the shiny objects with interest.

After spending time as a murder of crows, I know the appeal firsthand and can't judge.

Agents Tan and Roanhorse arrive with Archmage Doyle and a couple of apprentice mages.

"Do you think the angels will show?" agent Tan asks in her Bostonian accent.

Butterflies churn in my stomach, but I shrug. "If they don't, the council's banishment stands."

The room darkens, the candles flicker, and the floor shakes.

I fight not to roll my eyes as darkness spreads from a small point into a plume of black smoke, then grows to the size of a tree, expanding. A midnight fire churns at the center, likely to hide the spellwork involved.

Lucifer, flanked by fallen angels and demon guards, marches out. He's dressed as a king with all the luxury possible at his fingertips, replete with platinum and onyx crown. A sword gleams at his side and radiates with the light of an angel.

I've removed the hex from Lucifer's Grace. However, he won't allow me to do it for any other fallen. I can't breathe a word of what I've done to anyone else, either. Lucifer wants his brethren and minions alike to squirm, not knowing how he removed it.

Gabriel rolls his eyes.

The devil winks.

I told Lucifer I keep nothing from Gabriel and Phyr.

Not to be outdone, the leaders of the Angelic Anocracy appear in dazzling light and sparks. They're all in glittering white robes and their hair flows as if blown by a breeze. Unlike fae of all kinds of variety, none of the angels particularly stand out from one another in their white robes.

Some high fae flinch and low fae fly out of the way. Not my father, Oberon, who keeps his head as high and regal as Lucifer.

"Well, they won't get fired for not having enough flare," Rhiannon says out the corner of her mouth.

"I understood that reference," Phyr remarks. Ladle in hand, he returns to the kitchen.

This time, *I* roll my eyes.

Gabriel sidles next to me, his jaw clenched tight and every muscle tense. His gaze is centered on one angel. The Seraphim Gabriel, his father, is tall and pretty and, quite frankly, looks like the gold and diamond version of Lucifer's platinum and onyx vibe.

Their creator isn't very creative.

I take my Gabriel's hand in mine and give it a squeeze to say, "We've got this together."

He lifts our joined hands and kisses my fingers.

His father looks down his perfect angelic nose with disdain. Lucifer wears a similar expression, but it centers more on Gabriel. The nephil-shifter will never be good enough for me in the King of Hell's eyes, but I don't care.

Fae chaperone all the guests to their seats at the banquet table. The Supernatural Council of the Pacific Northwest are seated such that they can be viewed from any angle of the room. A little fae trickery there.

With all the guests seated, Gabriel calls everyone's attention. "Earth is but one world out of a myriad of inhabited worlds in the multiverse. It is small, and the mundanes are less advanced than in other places, but it is the world in which we choose to live." He gestures to the council. "Look at this table. None of us came from the same ancestry, nor do we share the same magic or beliefs, but we all get along. Why?"

"Community," I say.

He nods. "Community."

"A community is not vast," Leilani says. "Communities are where we live, work, and shop."

"It's where we raise our families," Aurora adds, smiling at Princess.

"We are here today to welcome you all to our community as guests," Gabriel continues.

I take my cue to speak. "We also want to warn you. If you have any designs on this place, we will assemble and unite against anyone who tries."

Agent Tan stands. "International Supernatural Enforcement Agency, the global mundane authority on all preternatural beings, recognizes the Supernatural Council of the Pacific Northwest as the acting, governing body for all matters of magic and will take their recommendation as to who is an enemy and who is an ally to mundane humans. Gabriel Crowfoot is recognized by the United Nations as an official ambassador for all Supernaturals. Any and all visas into this world will now be handled by him."

Judging Gabriel's father's face, the gravity of what Agent Tan says sinks in. Lucifer arches an eyebrow, gaze swinging in my direction. He's not mad, but he isn't happy either.

Both Heaven and Hell attended on the pretense that this would be a treaty negotiation. *Oopsy.*

"Whatever disagreements you have between your exterior groups will not be carried out on this world," agent Roanhorse adds. "If we hear otherwise from this council, the International Supernatural Enforcement Agency will make public the forty-year study about the effects of belief on your kind."

The entire ballroom falls silent.

Not one of us would be left unaffected.

So much rests on belief. Belief bestows on a magicless mundane the gifts of prophecy or persuasion, influencing masses. Belief makes an ordinary person a deity. Belief can strip a deity of their power, their very existence. For belief is a matter of the heart, not the mind, and what lies in the heart, whether it be strength, courage, love, or hate, is the most powerful magic of all.

EPILOGUE

I collect herbs from the garden, tying and placing them in a wicker basket. Jada and Rhiannon are helping with the harvest. Phyr is at the bakery, so it's just the three of us halfling witches.

P.C. weaves through my legs, marking me as his before moving on to chase a pixie. The little light sprites blip in and out of my garden, half their time spent in my faerie.

Rhiannon looks up from her work, "Do you wish you could have confronted your mother?"

I pause my work, taking a deep breath, truly considering the question. As of late, I've recognized Rhiannon asks questions with an intention in mind. Either she wants me to reflect on something I'd rather pass over, or she needs to figure something out about herself. We've both suffered losses —we heard through the coven grapevine that hers had died recently—she might need to work her own grief out.

I sigh. "I would like clarity about why she acted as she did toward her own flesh and blood, but what good would it do? The consequences of her actions would be the same. Any confrontation would only rouse old hurts better left in the past than reexamined."

Rhiannon wraps twine around some lavender cuttings, her face pensive. "My mother used to tell me I was her favorite wish and best hope. I wish I was the girl who still believed that."

My gaze turns to Jada. She's surrounded by the pixies, giggling as they play with her hair. Even after all that's happened, there's a bit of the innocent girl still left in the nineteen-year-old. Or perhaps she's simply resilient. I'd like to think the childhood Raf and I gave her provided that resilience.

"We can never return to the girl we were, Rhiannon, but we can break curses by not repeating the same mistakes our mothers made with the next generation."

She smiles. No. It's a full-on smirk. "Ah, so wise, Crone."

I cut her what I mean to be a sharp look, but I'm holding back my mirth. "I'm the Mother." I gesture to Jada as my evidence. "Besides, you're older than me."

She shrugs. "I may be fifty-seven and childless, but only Oberon knows how long your childhood in faerie lasted."

Mocking offence, I sniff and return to my work. A smile creeps up the corners of my mouth. I can't help it. Through her own actions, and later tragic demise, I may have lost my mother and coven, but this coven of three suits me just fine.

Acknowledgments

I'd like to thank my editors, Rhiannon Rhys-Jones and Emily Paper, my cover artist Les aka German creative, and my readers.

About the Author

T.J. Deschamps grew up in the Pennsylvania mountains where she learned the power of a vivid imagination and a good story. She now lives in Washington state in the suburbs of Seattle, a.k.a the Eastside. There she lives with her kids, cats, and tortoise, gardens badly, lifts weights, and drinks copious amounts of caffeine. She might be part dragon but is definitely a bog witch.

Follow her social media for updates, laughs, and fun.

www.ingramcontent.com/pod-product-compliance
Lightning Source LLC
Chambersburg PA
CBHW050403030726
47503CB00006B/2005